SUNRISE
OVER
FEATHER CREEK

Emma Lewis

I walked away from Elsa and never told her why. Now she's my only hope to save my animal sanctuary. Will she give me a second chance, or will my dreams go up in flames again?

After the devastating fire which destroyed the family animal sanctuary before it even opened, David and his sister are on the verge of being homeless. David has one chance to rekindle his dream of turning his failed ranch into a success. He must beg for the help of Elsa Ralston, his high school sweetheart. He left her before without a word before. Will she give him another chance and help him?
Elsa never expected to see David Jenner again after he broke her heart. Now he's back in her life, asking for money to save the farm where she had so many happy times. But as the new face of the Ralston Charitable Foundation, her hands are tied.
Will David forgive her?
David knows that second chances don't often come to guys like him. Elsa knows she's expected to toe the family line. Is it time for both of them to learn that the past doesn't need to shape their future?
Can they help each other heal their broken hearts as they watch the sun rise over
Feather Creek together?

Contents

Chapter 1

Davy

I woke to the sound of frantic barking, my heart thumping at the rude awakening. "Bailey, quiet!" I yelled, but the barking didn't stop for a second. In the darkness of my room, I frowned and pushed back the covers. Bailey was a blue heeler, an intelligent dog who thought he owned the farm and its humans. He wouldn't be barking for no reason. Maybe there were coyotes nearby.

I padded over to the window and peered out. Where there should be the complete darkness of the yard, I saw a yellow glow on the far side where our new animal sanctuary was ready and waiting for its first occupants. It took my sleepy brain a moment to catch up, then my heart stopped for a beat. The new building was lit up from inside. Did I forget to switch off the lights?

I peered closer. No, not the steady glow of electric light. This was too intense and moving. Realization pushed the sleep from me in an unwelcome rush. Flames! Our new sanctuary was on fire!

I tore out of my bedroom, yelling at the top of my voice. "Momma! Robyn! Wake up. The sanctuary is on fire!"

I heard sleepy responses from my momma and

sister, but I didn't stop to see if they were awake. No time to call the fire service. The sanctuary would be gone before the part-time officers reached the firehouse.

Bailey greeted me at the base of the stairs, still barking at top volume. I took a second to pat his head and ran into the yard. I stopped dead, rocking back on my heels. Even in the darkness I could see the sanctuary was beyond saving, flames now spread throughout the new building. Thick black smoke filled the yard. I could only give thanks there had been no animals in the kennels. The place wasn't due to open until next month.

"Oh no, Davy, what are we going to do?" Robyn coughed as she joined me.

"We've got to spray the house or we're going to lose it too," I yelled over the noise of the flames.

Momma appeared, a bandana covering her nose and mouth. "I'll take the horses into the paddock.

"Be careful in case the fire spreads," I warned, and she nodded.

Robyn and I headed to the small barns containing the hoses. I only hoped we had enough water in the bores to hold out.

At some point, neighbors from the farms north and east of us appeared, alerted by Momma, and they worked by our side in an attempt to contain the fire and save our home.

Dawn arrived, and still we didn't stop, but we were losing the battle against the voracious flames. It wouldn't take long before our home was gone too. Firefighters arrived just as I was losing hope, and finally the fire was brought under control, but it was too late to save the sanctuary and the barns around it.

I stood in the ashes of what would have been the office, my arms around my sister, Robyn, as she sobbed onto my chest, her copper-bright hair so like mine now covered in soot.

"I'm really sorry, Mrs. Jenner." Charlie Reedham, who had a ranch bordering north of ours, twisted his hat in his hands. He was as filthy as us.

"Thanks for helping," I said to him, holding out my soot-streaked hand.

He shook it, gave me a nod, and walked away to his old pick-up.

I turned back to the ruins of the sanctuary. My momma stood next to us, her hand on my shoulder, trying to comfort me. I should have been the one comforting her. Black Feather sanctuary was her dream. I had built it from scratch once we realized our sheep farm was failing, a promise of a new beginning. I surveyed what was left. The fire had left nothing but the charred remains of my family's dreams.

Six months later

"I'm not going to do it." I slammed my fist down onto the kitchen table. Everything jumped or rattled, and the pepper shaker fell over and rolled off, but neither of us paid any attention to it.

Robyn flinched but the resolute expression on her face didn't change. "It's our only chance of keeping the farm, Davy."

I scowled at her. "I'm not going to beg."

"Then Black Feather farm is finished, and you'd better go pack because we're gonna be homeless soon."

I slammed out of the kitchen door and stood on the stoop. Bailey, the heeler, wandered over to see how I was. I dug my fingers into the dog's fur as I tried to bring my anger under control. I wasn't angry at Robyn, not really, but at the circumstances that brought us here. I could barely look at the charred patch of ground where the sanctuary had been for such a short time. The fire had been caused by an electrical short-circuit, thanks to a curious rodent. Nothing I could have done would have prevented the blaze.

The door opened behind me, but I didn't turn around to look. My sister was only going to yell at me again. To my surprise, she laid a gentle hand on my shoulder, just as my momma would have done. She didn't say anything. At twenty-four and two years younger than me, she had a wise head on her shoulders. Without my little sister I'd have done something stupid months ago. I didn't tell her that, but I think she knew.

I sighed, blinked back tears, and stared up at the endless blue sky. "It's so unfair."

"I know." Her voice was soft.

"Momma was finally going to have what she always wanted."

"I know."

"We planned for this for years."

Robyn didn't bother to say, "I know," again.

"We lost her when we needed her most," I said quietly.

Our momma had died the week after the fire. The official cause of death was a cardiac arrest, but we both knew she'd died of a broken heart. We'd laid her to rest beside our daddy and mourned our loss.

Six months on, we'd done our best to work out how to rebuild the sanctuary, but the bank was getting impatient, and our options were running out. They'd run out months back, but neither of us wanted to believe it. The farm had been on its knees before the fire. The prolonged cold of the previous winter had been its death knell. We'd kept a few sheep, rare breeds I didn't want to sell, but the farm I remembered as a child was long gone.

"I can't go begging to *him*."

"You're not asking him. You're asking the Ralston Foundation for help to rebuild the sanctuary. The old man probably won't even be there. I doubt anyone will know who we are."

"We can't afford the tickets," I said stubbornly. "They're a thousand dollars a head."

"You looked it up, huh?"

Yeah, I'd looked at the Ralston Foundation website and that was when I'd put two and two together.

She sighed and squeezed my shoulder. "Aunt Livvy is paying for us to go. She's the one who suggested we try the Boston gala fundraiser in the first place."

"They won't give us any help," I snapped.

"There are big names chasing funding. Why would they help a non-profit on a tiny farm that's being foreclosed?"

"Because the Ralstons are a big name here and besides, do we have any choice?"

I tilted my head to glower at my sister, stubbornly refusing to answer.

Robyn buried her face in my hair and her arm went around my neck. "If we wanna stay here, you've got to swallow your pride, Davy."

It had been a long time since I had been around so many people. Not since high school, and apart from the prom I didn't go to, none of them had been dressed in tuxedos or, in the women's cases, long slinky dresses and killer heels I didn't want anywhere near my feet. We entered the ballroom of Ralston House and stared at the sparkling tableau in front of them.

Robyn choked as a woman walked past in a silver dress.

"What's the matter?" I asked, tugging at the bow tie which was strangling me.

"I'm not retying for you," Robin warned. "And what that woman was wearing around her neck cost more than we owe the bank."

I grimaced. I wasn't usually bothered about how much money other people had compared to me, but tonight it was like a slap in the face. Probably the outfits most of the women wore would pay what we owed the bank. It was as if we were the poor kids standing at the window while the rich people played.

Robyn clutched at my arm. I looked down at her. She stared wide-eyed at the people around her.

I patted her hand. "Hey, what's the matter?"

"You're right. We shouldn't be here."

"You're the one who said this was our only choice."

"I know. This was before I saw all these beautiful people. We're like the poor relations." Robyn looked ready to bolt.

"The only difference between them and us is a couple of million in the bank," I scoffed, ignoring the fact I'd had exactly the same thoughts only seconds before.

"That's all?" She forced a smile, and I appreciated the effort.

"That's all," I confirmed.

Robyn barked out a laugh and people turned around to look at us. "Well, in that case...."

"Let's go and find our seats," I suggested.

"They've probably put us in the kitchen," she muttered darkly.

Before we could move, there was a wave of clapping. We turned to see people moving to the top table on the dais.

My stomach roiled. These were the people I had to schmooze, to beg for the chance to rebuild my sanctuary, to stay on my family's land. I'd practiced my pitch over and over at Robyn until she agreed I was good enough. Now my confidence crumbled in the face of the expensive suits. I watched them file across the dais, five men and four women. All of them with the potential to destroy my life with one simple word. I studied the woman who was guided to the center seat. I'd expected old man Ralston. She was young and pretty, with glossy red hair swept behind her, dressed in midnight blue silk. I stiffened, closed my eyes, and prayed really hard. I opened them again. The woman with the glossy red hair was still there, smiling as her companion pulled out her chair. She didn't have a care in the world. I saw the sapphires around her slender neck. Any one of those gems would have saved my sanctuary.

Robyn clutched at me again. "Davy! That woman in the middle of the table. Isn't she...?"

"It's Elsa Ralston," I said dully.

Life really knew how to kick a man when he was down.

"Elle. It's Elle." She was so wide-eyed it was almost comical.

"Yeah."

"The love of your life you walked away from without telling her the truth."

"Shout a bit louder," I said sourly. "You can tell the whole room I dumped the woman who holds the purse strings."

Maybe I was the one talking too loudly because a couple of people nearby gave me a sideways glance.

"Let's go home before this night gets any worse," I muttered.

"Okay."

That was why I loved my little sister. She always had my back in any situation.

I turned to leave but couldn't resist a last glance at Elsa. She was looking directly at me as if she'd seen a ghost. But she couldn't have seen me in this crowd of people.

Why did it have to be Elle? The girl I'd loved with all my heart and walked away from. If I had to put aside my pride and beg, why did it have to be her?

"Davy?" Robyn touched my shoulder. "Are you ready?"

"Yeah, let's go."

I tugged at the collar and bow tie again. I needed to get out of here. It was suffocating me.

Chapter 2

Elle

I studied my reflection in the long ornate mirror. "I look like a trussed-up turkey." The girl in the mirror looked amazing, but she wasn't me.

The woman standing behind me scoffed. "Don't be ridiculous, Elsa. You look wonderful. It's so good to see you clean for once."

"Thanks, Mom," I said dryly. "You know how to make a girl feel good."

My mother waved a cream silk-clad hand. "You know what I mean."

I did, but I didn't need to be reminded that I was usually wearing a layer of dirt from bandana to boots. I was a landscape gardener. My usual uniform was T-shirt, flannels and pants or shorts. The last time I'd worn a dress was graduation from high school. Now I was clad in a midnight-blue silk designer dress, my red hair professionally dressed and my make-up perfect. I may have looked amazing on the outside, but on the inside, I was a mess of nerves. Still, it was my mom and I had to poke the hornets' nest.

"Turkey," I declared because I felt uncomfortable in my skin. "And do I have to wear these heels? It's a long dress, they won't see my boots."

The blue velvet mules were beautiful, but I longed for my comfortable work boots. I could hide them under the dress.

"It's one night," my mother said with exasperation. "Just one night. You can make the effort. Put your gloves on. Your hands are still so rough. Do you even remember to use the cream I gave you?"

I bit back the angry words. My hands were work-roughened because I was a gardener, not a fashion accessory. I knew my mother meant well but I was so tired of being told to, "Stand up straight, dear, and for goodness sake, smile. You're a Ralston. It's expected of you now."

I've always been a Ralston. But there was a difference between being a Ralston and *the* Ralston. In Texas and Boston, people said my name in the same way they spoke about a queen. Not long ago, I'd been Elle Ralston, landscape gardener in Ohio, where no one cared about my name, and slowly building up my own business. Then my grandfather died. He was the patriarch of the Ralston empire, a formidable man I had loved dearly. I don't know why he chose me, but overnight I became *the* Elsa Ralston, heir to his fortune. I was a billionairess, and my little business in Ohio was sold. Nobody asked me if that's what I wanted. I was a Ralston, and family came first.

In addition, I was also the patron and face of the Ralston Foundation which gave grants to good works. Which was why I was here tonight—under protest—for the fundraising fall gala.

Elle who loved digging out ponds and laying paths had been left behind. In her place was Elsa, plucked, pampered and unhappy. I wasn't sure I liked this girl. Her smile was fake. She wasn't easy-go-lucky, laughing Elle.

My father, who had sensibly stayed out of the discussion, came up behind me. "I have something for you."

I caught his gaze in the mirror, raising one 'perfectly arched now it was plucked to within an inch of its life' eyebrow. "A pony?" I clapped my hands. "Tell me it's a pony, Papa."

My mom tsked and stalked away, her heels clicking across the floor as she radiated disapproval. I loved my mom dearly, but she never understood how she got a daughter who preferred digging flower beds to dancing and drinking champagne.

My father's lips twitched but he managed to maintain a straight face. "Not today, pumpkin." He held out a sapphire necklace. "The Ralston Sapphires."

"I'd rather have a pony," I said.

"You can buy yourself as many ponies as you want now," he pointed out as he placed the deep blue gems around my neck and stood back to study me. "Perfect. You look beautiful."

The gems matched my dress perfectly and made my blue eyes even deeper.

"If I sell the necklace I could buy even more." I was more interested in the ponies than how I looked.

"Elsa!"

I grimaced at my mother's shriek of outrage. I loved my mom, but we were like chalk and cheese. With my elevation in the family, my mom was thrilled she could take part in all the pomp and ceremony that came with being a Ralston, whereas I wanted to run back to Ohio. I knew I was a disappointment to my mother. Jennifer had wanted a little girl she could dress up and play with. Instead, I had spent all my childhood growing plants, building ponds, and riding with my friends who lived on a farm. I spent more time there than I did at home.

I looked at my father's deep blue eyes, almost identical to my own, in the mirror. His red hair was fading now, but once it had been as dark as mine. "I'm going to have to apologize, aren't I?"

He kissed the top of my head. "Peace is always a good idea."

I sighed. "Let's go play nice."

"Good girl," he chuckled. "Remember, it's just one night."

"Of the rest of my life," I grumbled.

I deeply missed my simple life back in Ohio, but I could never return.

The Ralston Foundation had been my grandmother's baby. She had been a beautiful socialite but with a strong work ethic and helping charities had been her raison d'etre. When she had passed away, my grandfather kept the foundation going and it was more successful than ever.

Tonight's ball was the biggest fundraising exercise of the year, with an auction full of donated first-class prizes, but also a chance for smaller nonprofits to network with the foundation committee during the evening. Privately, I thought if they could afford the tickets to the gala maybe they didn't need the grants, but I was sensible enough to keep that from my mother.

"Deep breath," my father said as he opened the door to the ballroom. "You're the belle of the ball tonight. Everyone is going to want to talk to you."

"Remember to smile. Stand up straight. They're here to see Elsa Ralston," my mom instructed.

"Yes, Mom." I forced a smile and held my head high, winning an approving nod.

Elsa Ralston. Elsa Ralston.

I wondered if I could change my name between now and going through the door.

My father squeezed my hand. "You'll be fine, pumpkin."

I hoped so. This was so close to my childhood nightmare of standing in front of my class and discovering I was wearing no pants. I could still hear the mocking dream-laughter now.

The ballroom was a cacophony of sounds and light; music and chatter assaulting the senses, then a ripple of applause as people realized the committee were taking their seats. I wanted to run, but instead I let myself be led to the center of the table on the dais. I was the star turn for the evening and I needed to act like it.

I sat down, smiling at a few people I knew. Men in tuxedos and women in flowing gowns made their way to the tables. There were still a few people around the edges, and one caught my attention. A flame in a sea of black tuxedos. A tall man with bright red hair, so like my own. The breath caught in my throat and my vision blurred for a moment. I blinked, sure he'd be gone when I opened my eyes, but he was still there. It couldn't be, not after all this time.

I hadn't seen him in nearly ten years. Davy Jenner, my high school sweetheart, my best friend in school and the boy I was convinced I'd spend the rest of my life with. Davy Jenner, the man who walked out on me when I needed him most.

I studied him closely. He'd filled out in the decade since I last saw him. I could see the outline of his broad shoulders and muscled arms straining the seams of the ill-fitting tux. His fiery hair glinted under the harsh light of the chandeliers, and he needed a closer shave. He tugged at his collar, and I had to smile. Davy looked as ill at ease in his finery as I did.

A red-haired woman in a pale green dress touched his arm. I went cold. He was married or at least attached? Davy had brought his wife here. For what? To flaunt their happiness in front of me. I knew it was ridiculous even as I wondered if he knew I was here. Then I caught sight of her face and my anger died as quickly as it had flared. That was Davy's little sister, Robyn. She'd grown up into a beautiful woman. As if she knew someone was watching her, Robyn looked across the room and saw me. I could see the shock on her face.

Don't tell him. Please don't tell him.

But of course Robyn did and he turned to look

at me. Our gazes locked and his shock and dismay were evident even from here.

I hope you feel bad after what you did to me.

What was he doing here? How could he have afforded the tickets? The Jenners had never had any money. I couldn't imagine the situation had changed since I'd last seen them. They'd lived on a rundown farm in the middle of Texas. I had loved visiting Black Feather farm. It was one of the few times I felt I could breathe, away from the stifling life my mom wanted for me. Davy and Robyn had been my best friends and Davy's momma had treated me like one of her kids. I thrived under her care. She'd never cared about how filthy I was as long as I brought clean hands to the table. Losing Davy's family had been almost as hard as losing Davy. They had been my family too.

I felt the anger building inside me again. He'd walked away from me without a backward glance. I snorted as he turned away. Again. Typical.

My father leaned toward me, a look of concern on his face. "Elle, is everything okay?"

I forced a smile. "I'm fine, Daddy."

But I couldn't resist a last glance at the man who broke my heart. He'd turned at the door to stare at me. We locked gazes across the ballroom. I wondered if he knew how much he'd hurt me by walking away from me. I wondered if he cared.

Chapter 3

Davy

I tore my gaze away from Elle's and hurried out of the huge doors that led to the ballroom. Robyn waited for me, her gaze almost pitying. I averted my eyes. Robyn was my best friend as well as my beloved little sister, but I didn't need her pity.

The hatcheck girl smiled at us quizzically as Robyn handed over the tickets for our coats.

"Leaving before dinner?"

"Uh, yeah, family emergency," Robyn said.

"That's a shame. The food is always amazing at a Ralston event. It'll be a pity to miss it." The girl sounded sincere which was nice, but I'd rather have eaten dust than anything the Ralstons provided.

I shrugged into my coat and helped Robyn on with hers over her borrowed dress. I hoped we could call a car because Robyn wasn't used to wearing heels, even small ones. I turned to ask the hatcheck girl, but there was a polite cough behind me.

"Mr. Jenner?"

I was faced with the thinnest man I had ever seen. He was, I guessed, in his sixties, silver-gray hair and wispy on top. He was a similar height to me, but I could have made three of him.

I forced a smile. "Yes, I'm David Jenner."

"I'm Brian Marsden, I work for the Ralston Foundation. Ms. Ralston asks for a few minutes of your time. She would like to speak to you."

No way! My smile turned into more of a grimace.

"I'm sorry, but we have to go. Family emergency," I lied.

Marsden inclined his head. "I understand, but she would like to talk to you about the sanctuary."

I was about to decline again because the last thing I wanted was to be in the same room as Elle Ralston, but Robyn tugged at my arm. I scowled down at her.

Her glare was just as forceful. "Davy, this is why we're here. To talk to people about the sanctuary. We need help, remember?"

"But not from her," I said. "Never her."

Then I grimaced, remembering one of Elle's employees was standing next to me. I glanced his way. Marsden still wore the bland smile. I inhaled and tried to calm my nerves at the thought of talking to the woman I had loved again. "Okay. We can spare a few minutes."

Robyn dug me in the ribs and smiled at Marsden. "What my ungracious brother means is we'd be delighted to talk to Elle, I mean Ms. Ralston."

Marsden kept his face impassive, but I swore I saw a twinkle in his eye. "Please follow me."

We followed him down a short hallway and

into a small room, each wall covered with shelves of books floor to ceiling. From the muted sound of chatter, I guessed it led off the ballroom. If I hadn't been so nervous, I might have checked out the books. They looked well read rather than for show.

Marsden turned to us. "Please wait here. Ms. Ralston will be with you as soon as possible."

Then he left us alone to stare at each other. There was a scattering of applause from the ballroom on the other side of the wall. I stared at the wall as though I'd suddenly developed x-ray vision.

"It'll be all right, Davy."

I turned to look at my sister again. "What?"

She gave me an oddly tender smile. That made me more nervous than if she'd shouted at me. Robyn wasn't known for her tenderness.

"It'll be all right. She just wants to talk to us about the sanctuary, nothing else."

"How does she know about the sanctuary?" I demanded. "It wasn't built when she...knew us."

Robyn snorted as I stumbled over my words. "I imagine she looked at the guest list. When I bought the tickets, I had to tick the box about our nonprofit and what help we were looking for. Elle knows us and the farm. She was probably curious why we were here. I mean, we don't fit in with the rich and famous, do we?"

It was my turn to give a derisive snort. "I've got nothing in common with anyone out there. I don't suppose any of them have lifted a finger to do an honest day's work in their life."

I saw Robyn's expression change from rolling her eyes to opening them so wide it was almost comical.

The voice behind me shouldn't have been a surprise.

"That's where you'd be wrong."

I closed my eyes. I could have stepped back a decade, to a couple of teenagers laying on the flatbed of a truck, holding hands under the stars. I turned to face the girl who had haunted my dreams forever. She wasn't a girl any longer. She was a beautiful woman, apart from her scowl which was as fierce as mine.

"Still carrying that chip on your shoulder about rich people, Davy?" she said. "Not every rich person lays on a chaise longue and demands servants peel them grapes."

Opening salvo fired. And reminding me of a conversation we'd had many years ago when I'd been railing against the injustice of my family living hand-to-mouth while others—I'd never mentioned Elle's family, but she wasn't stupid— threw money away like water. Elle was going to play dirty. Well, two could play at that game.

I arched an eyebrow. "Says the richest person in the room. How many servants do you have?"

"We call them staff and they get well paid," she said, her tone like ice. "At least they are loyal."

Reminding me that I wasn't. I'd done the walking.

"Well, this is fun," Robyn murmured. "Do you want me to get a couple of knives and you can continue to slice each other up, or are we going to get down to business?"

Elsa blushed as she turned to my sister. "I'm sorry, Robyn, that was rude of me. I should have said hello before we started the fight. It's good to see *you* again."

Robyn waved a hand. "It's fine, Elle. Davy drives us all to murderous rage."

"Thanks," I muttered. She was supposed to be on my side.

She ignored me and walked over to Elsa to hug her. Then she pulled back. "We can still do this, yes?"

Elsa rolled her eyes. "I'm still Elle."

I watched her hug my little sister. Under all the trappings of finery, she was still the girl I'd fallen in love with.

"Well, yes and no." Robyn pointed at the necklace. "I don't remember you wearing rocks like that when you dug out our pond."

Elsa touched the necklace like she'd forgotten it was there. "I asked for a pony. They made me wear this instead."

Robyn furrowed her brow. "Huh?"

"Never mind." Elsa took a deep breath. "I was surprised to see you here."

Robyn looked over her shoulder at me. I shrugged. In contrast to me, if we were going to have to beg for money, Robyn would rather it was to Elsa than a total stranger. Elsa had been family for most of our lives. Before Robyn could launch into our story there was a rap at the door.

"Yes?" Elsa called out,

"Ms. Ralston?"

"Who does he expect it to be?" she muttered. "Yes?"

"You're expected back in the ballroom."

She grimaced. "I'm sorry, I have to go back."

"We'll talk to you another time," Robyn suggested.

Elsa shook her head. "Come back in. You've got seats and you paid for your tickets. You may as well benefit from the dinner. As soon as I've done my party piece, we can talk about the sanctuary."

I was about to decline because the last thing I wanted to do was spend the evening making awkward small talk with strangers, but Robyn smiled and nodded.

"Deal. It's so good to see you again, Elle."

Elsa smiled and took Robyn's hands. "You were a kid last time I saw you, and now look at you."

"It's been too long."

Although I couldn't see Robyn's face, I could tell by the quaver in her voice that she was holding back tears.

"Yes, it has," Elsa agreed and her eyes gleamed suspiciously bright.

The knock came again, more forceful this time. "Ms. Ralston."

I caught the exasperation on Elsa's face. "Yes?"

"They are waiting for you in the ballroom."

Elsa huffed and I swear I heard her mutter something about handcuffs. "I have to go, or Mom will yell at me. I'll see you afterward?"

Robyn looked over her shoulder at me and the pleading in her expression was plain to see. She wanted to reconnect with Elle again. Despite my misgivings, I nodded, and she turned back to Elsa. "We'll see you afterward. Can't pass up the chance of a good dinner."

Elsa smiled at Robyn then flicked a glance my way. I saw the relief in her eyes and realized she was as anxious as Robyn to catch up. "Make sure you don't miss out," she agreed. "The food is good here."

She smiled again and vanished out of the room with a soft swish of her dress, contrasting with the quiet click of her heels. I heard her apologizing to someone for keeping them waiting. Elsa always had been polite.

Robyn let out an explosive breath and turned back to me. "Well, Davy, we might be able to save the sanctuary yet."

"Just because Elle wants to talk to us doesn't mean to say she has any interest in the sanctuary, or that the Foundation will deign to give us a grant." I didn't want to spoil her pleasure in meeting Elsa again, but she needed to keep her feet on the ground.

Her face took on a stubborn expression which I recognized. "She loved the farm. Of course she'll want to help."

I didn't want to crush her dreams. We had lost so much since the fire. If we lost the farm too, I didn't know what we'd do. We had no other family except Aunt Livvy, my mom's sister, and she lived in a tiny one-story in a large town five hours away from us. Our backup plan had gone up in flames. We had nothing left.

"Mr. Jenner? Ms. Jenner?"

I looked over to see Brian Marsden smiling at us.

"Ms. Ralston asked me to escort you into dinner."

"Making sure you don't run away," Robyn muttered as we followed him out of the room.

I said nothing. My sister knew me far too well. And it seemed, so did Elsa.

Chapter 4

Elle

I followed Brian Marsden down the hall, a grim-faced, muscular bodyguard at my back. I was amused at the bodyguard's sudden arrival. Did Brian think he might have to force me to leave the room or worse, I was in danger from the Jenners?

I had been in danger but not the sort he must have imagined. It was my heart that was in danger of breaking again. The blood pounded so loud in my ears I was amazed the two men couldn't hear it.

Davy Jenner. I'd been in the same room as Davy Jenner.

Even if we had spent most of our time sniping at each other. That had almost been fun. He was still as prickly and adorable as ever, with a chip on either shoulder where wealth was concerned. My amusement faded away. It was easy to laugh when money wasn't an issue. The Jenners were probably living hand-to-mouth now.

Davy had been handsome as a teenager, with muscles from working long hours on the farm, hair the color of a blazing fire, and eyes so dark green they seemed almost black in some lights. I'd always found him more interesting than the jocks at our high school. They strutted about; over-muscled, girls hanging over their arms, dripping with testosterone. Davy on the other hand had the physique of a man who worked hard. The girls didn't give him a second glance. He didn't have the status or the money to interest them. I'd heard the whispered, "Farm boy," flung after him more than once. Davy didn't seem to notice, until one day I saw his jaw clench and I realized every barb found its target. From that moment I'd done my best to protect him from the bullying. It was years later when I discovered he'd done the same for me. My family name was no protection against the bullies.

Now Davy was twice the size with broad shoulders and a slim waist; even in the ill-fitting suit I could see his broad chest and long legs. Despite his fair skin it was tanned from long hours in the sun, a fan of faint lines in the corner of his eyes.

I pressed my lips together. I had to get a grip. It didn't matter that my childhood sweetheart, my best friend, had just walked back into my life. It didn't matter he'd turned into a stunningly handsome man. When I'd needed him most, he hadn't been there. I swallowed around the lump in my throat and blinked rapidly to force away the tears. My mother would kill me if I wrecked the carefully applied make-up.

The ballroom was awash with noise. It was overwhelming for a moment. I wanted to run, and I knew Davy, who preferred the quiet of his farm to crowds of people, must be on the verge of bolting. But I followed Marsden through the crowd, politely greeting people as they came up to me and promising a longer conversation later. One person I expected to be here appeared to be absent. Lily Duchamp was an old friend I'd seen on the guest list and had looked forward to catching up with her. Her parents were here, but there was no sign of Lily.

I tapped Marsden's shoulder. "Brian, sorry, could you find out if Lily Duchamp is here?"

"Certainly." He turned but I caught Marsden's arm before he left. He glanced at me, surprise on his face.

I gave him an apologetic smile. "Please could you escort Mr. and Ms. Jenner to their table first. Before he makes a run for the exit."

"Of course," he said without a hint of a smile, and vanished back the way he'd come.

My mother scowled at me as I reached the dais, to be quickly smoothed away and replaced by a polished smile. I sighed. I was going to pay for my disappearing act. Did my mother know who I'd gone to talk to? Most likely she did. Marsden was my mother's puppet. No. that was unfair. I liked the older man, but his loyalties did lie with the Ralston Family™, the latter added sarcastically in my mind.

"Where have you been?" my mom snapped as I sat down. "We were going to have to start without you."

"I'm sure you'd have managed splendidly," I said as blandly as I could. I caught my father's pleading look and sighed. Edward Ralston, a bear in the boardroom, was thoroughly under his wife's thumb. He wanted me to play nice. "I went to talk to the owners of an animal sanctuary," I said.

Mom's face softened a fraction. "That's kind of you, dear, but you know the Foundation has already picked out its causes for the year."

I frowned. "Then why are we hosting this gala?"

"To raise funds for the foundation." My mother spoke as if I were a child.

"We're taking money from the very people who need our help."

"And they may get help, in future years."

"But that will be too late—"

I'd lost my mother's attention, claimed by the major domo.

"Too late for whom?" my father asked.

"For the smaller charities," I said lamely.

I looked out over the ballroom, seeking Davy and Robyn, finding them easily thanks to their flame-colored hair at a table near the back of the room. I couldn't see their faces. Did they know this was a waste of their time? That they'd have been better saving their money? Obviously not or Davy wouldn't have been here, I was sure of that.

"Pumpkin?"

I turned to see my father's curious gaze. "I just don't think it's fair, is all. I don't mean the larger charities, but the smaller nonprofits in real need. They need to know they have no chance of us helping them now."

Edward sighed and nodded. "I used to think the same way, but your grandmother felt the foundation was better designed to help the larger charitable organizations."

My lip curled. "More publicity for the foundation, you mean."

My father didn't answer. He didn't need to. I knew how the system worked. It's what I'd been trying to get away from for my whole life. Money went to money. Thousands of dollars would be chaneled into high profile charities, or whatever was the celebrity-driven charity of the week, while the tiny operations in real need would sink without a trace. Like Black Feather Farm.

"It's the way it is," my father said.

"Yes."

It was, but I didn't have to like the hypocrisy of it. I was the face of the Foundation now. There had to be something I could do.

The evening seemed endless to me, and the only thing that kept my attention was the man on the other side of the room. It was easy to see Davy and Robyn sat in uncomfortable silence, ignored by the other people on their table. It was school all over again. I gritted my teeth at the way they were being treated.

The five-course meal was superb, the Ralston Foundation didn't stint on wooing the rich and powerful for their donations, but it could have been ramen for all I cared, and I noticed Davy barely ate.

The speeches started, my father giving a culogy for my grandfather and assuring everyone that the foundation would continue with its good works under the leadership of the new CEO, his daughter, Elsa Ralston. The applause was huge.

A spotlight turned on me. I swallowed hard. Deer in headlights all the way.

"Smile," Jennifer hissed at me.

I forced a smile on my face, stood on unsteady legs, and joined my father at the podium. I was now the public face of the Ralston Foundation whether I wanted to be or not. All eyes were upon me, but I was really only conscious of the burning green eyes from the back of the crowded room.

My mother had forced a prepared speech into my hands just before we'd walked into the ballroom. I had skimmed it. The sad loss of my grandfather, my promise to be a steady hand at the reins with the guidance of my parents, praise for the charities it had supported, and then a list of the worthy causes the Foundation would support over the coming year.

I could do this. Dry mouth or not, this was my role in the family business. There was no son and heir to carry on the empire, only a daughter, and I had to do my part. I'd heard the 'only' for most of my life, my mother always keen to tell me how much easier it would have been if I'd been a son.

I started to read the speech my mother had prepared, willing my voice not to shake. I'd spoken in public before, I was a Ralston after all. But really I was speaking to one man, trying to explain why my family's foundation wouldn't be able to help him. I could see the exact point he realized he was wasting his time, and worse, I caught the same look of betrayal on Robyn's face. They had come looking for help and instead found nothing except a good meal and an understanding of just how far down the food chain they were.

I kept talking until the end of the speech. There was a pause, then loud clapping from everyone except the two people I desperately wanted to help. Other members of the committee came up to thank me and kiss me on the cheek, and when I turned back to the crowd, my eyes seeking the back of the room, I wasn't surprised to discover their seats were empty.

Chapter 5

Davy

I stormed down the stone steps of the mansion, impatiently waiting at the foot for Robyn to join me. She'd remembered to collect our coats from the hatcheck girl a second time. I was steaming, the chill Fall air barely making a dent in my anger. I could have left my jacket behind and not felt the cold.

I'd hoped...for one foolish moment after our conversation...that Elsa would help us. That our relationship had meant something. That she cared about the survival of Black Feather farm and the animal sanctuary. But it all meant nothing to her. My family were just performing animals for people like the Ralstons. The gala was nothing but a sham. We'd sat there, hoping against hope our little nonprofit would be picked while all the money was destined to big name charities. And what did we get? Dinner and disappointment.

I smacked my fist into the wall. Pain shot through my arm, but my anger was so fierce I barely felt it.

"That was a stupid thing to do," Robyn snapped as she negotiated the steps in her high heels. "Let me look at your hand. Is anything broken?"

"Only my heart," I muttered, obediently showing her my bruised and bloodied knuckles.

Robyn took my hand, gently flexing each finger. "Elle broke your heart a long time ago, Davy. Maybe you have a second chance now."

"She's a Ralston and I'm a Jenner," I snarled. "There are no second chances for the likes of us."

Robyn sighed. "Elle has just been shoehorned into the role, Davy. You didn't think that maybe she had no choice? That the foundation had already decided where the money was going before she knew we were there?"

"Then why did we bother, Robyn? If you knew that already why drag me here and put me through this?" I stared at her, betrayed that she'd made me confront Elle Ralston again. Robyn knew how much I'd loved her.

Robyn let go of my hand and looked away. "Because I hoped when she saw you that she'd help us no matter what had been decided."

"Look how well that turned out," I muttered. "Let's go back to the motel."

"We'll go home tomorrow, Davy," Robyn sighed. "Forget about the Ralstons. There has to be an answer somewhere."

I wrapped my arm around her shoulders. "You're the best sister in the world."

Robyn rested her head on my shoulder. "I'm the only one you've got, doofus."

I was so lucky to have my little sister. Even if she did call me a doofus.

"I just want to be home," she admitted. "I hate this place."

"Me too, Robyn," I said, holding her close to me. "Me too."

I loved the farm with every fiber of my being. If only going home didn't mean facing homelessness.

A week later I was out repairing the fences on the south side of the farm. Just because we'd be out on our ear didn't mean to say I could quit with the repairs and sit on my ass all day. I took pleasure in the repetitive tasks. Who knew what I'd end up doing once the farm was gone? It kept me awake at night. I wasn't qualified to do anything else but farming. I barely finished high school and there had been no money for us to go to college. Robyn kept telling me I should network and see if there were any vacancies in the local area for ranch hands. I asked why I couldn't phone them. She laughed at me until tears rolled down her cheeks. That was why she worked on the computer, and I dealt with the critters. I wasn't qualified for jack.

I was lost in my thoughts, which kept returning to Elle, when my phone buzzed.

"I'm not finished yet," I said when I connected the call.

"You need to come back here, Davy," Robyn said. Her voice sounded weird.

Concern flooded through me. The last time she'd sounded like that was when Momma died. Had the hammer fallen? Were the bailiffs here already? "What's wrong?"

"Just get your ass back here," she snapped.

I snorted. That sounded more like her, and the tension subsided a fraction. "Gonna be at least an hour. I've got to fix this hole, or we'll have more breakouts." I swore the fence broke every week no matter how often I repaired it.

"'Kay."

She disconnected but before she did, I heard her talking to someone. She sounded relaxed so maybe it was old Mrs. Thompson. She had been Momma's best friend and she liked to visit occasionally. She'd never give us any warning which drove Robyn nuts because she was always the one left entertaining Mrs. Thompson until I got back to the house. I didn't mind the old girl. She could be abrasive and undiplomatic, but she'd loved Momma and mourned her passing as much as we did.

I finished the fencing despite Robyn's order, because I couldn't leave it as it was. That took me another thirty minutes or more. By the time I rode into the yard, it was almost six o'clock and over two hours since she called me. I wasn't surprised when Robyn rushed out of the door ready to scold me.

"I'm tired, Raindrop needs a rub down, and I need a shower," I said as she opened her mouth. "Can you just tell me why you called me back?"

"Why don't you let me take care of Raindrop?" a light voice said behind me.

I glared at Robyn. She was too busy smirking at me to be cowed.

I turned to face Elsa. No, she was my Elle, dressed in a green cotton shirt and tight jeans. No designer dresses and jewelry. The change made me blink. "What are you doing here?"

"I'm sorry about my brother, Elle," Robyn said. "He keeps forgetting his manners."

"I'm sorry," I muttered. Then I spotted the black-clad men walking into the yard. I scowled. "What are they doing here?"

Elle laid a hand on my arm. "Taking care of me. Go take a shower, Davy. I'll look after Raindrop. She's a lovely old girl," she cooed, patting Raindrop's neck.

"I can take care of my own horse," I snapped, anger bubbling inside me again. Then I caught Elle's kicked puppy expression and I deflated like a pricked balloon. Whatever had happened to us, it wasn't Elle's fault. I took a deep breath and forced a smile. "Thanks, Elle. I know she'll appreciate it. I'll go take a shower."

Before I make even more of an idiot of myself.

I strode into the house, leaving the two girls in the yard. The door closed behind them, but not before I heard Robyn apologize to Elle for my behavior again.

I had to get my anger under control if I was going to have any kind of civil conversation with Elle. I'd always been quick to temper, and it faded just as quickly. But since the sanctuary fire and my mom's passing, it was as if the anger in me never died away, and anything would set me blazing again. Despair did that to a person.

"You're being an ass," Robyn said bluntly, glowering at me in the doorway of my bedroom.

I sat down on the bed. "I know."

Robyn looked taken aback. She had obviously been prepared for a fight. "Why are you treating Elle like this. She's our *friend*. And we don't have many friends left, Davy."

"I know."

In fairness, Robyn and I had never had many friends. We'd been considered the weird kids at high school. But then so had Elle. That's why she'd fitted in so well with us. Losing her had left a hole in our lives which had never gotten filled. As well as a hole in my heart.

Robyn sighed as she sat down next to me and took my hand. "You've got to listen to her, Davy. She didn't come all the way out here to talk to me. She'd have called me. Elle wants to talk to you. You have to listen."

"Will it save the farm?"

She shrugged. "How do I know? But Elle's our friend, and we owe her that at least."

I looked at my little sister. "When did you get so wise?"

She knocked her head on my shoulder. "Someone has to keep you in check. I'm going to find Elle. Hurry up with your shower. I want to know why she's here as much as you do."

She left me then, alone with my thoughts. My sister was right. I owed it to Elle to listen.

Chapter 6

Elle

I crooned to the mare as I brushed her coat, working out the dust and knots. She snuffled and nuzzled me as if she remembered me from before. I don't know if she did, but the way she leaned against me was comforting. I felt more at home here than I had since the moment I received the news that I'd inherited the Ralston empire.

I sighed and rested my forehead against Raindrop's soft neck. "Why does he hate me so much, Raindrop? What did I do?"

I hadn't expected Davy to welcome me with open arms, but his anger was hard to deal with. He'd been an open, happy teenager, content to be on the farm with parents who loved him. I'd envied his happy home life so much. It's why I spent so much time here. I pretended to myself I'd become another Jenner kid. Momma Jenner treated me the same way she treated her kids.

"You didn't do anything," Robyn said.

I looked over Raindrop. Robyn rested her arms on the stall door, her red hair tumbling around her shoulders.

"Then what happened, Robyn? Because I really don't know."

She pressed her lips together. "You should ask Davy."

"Will he give me a straight answer or will he shout at me and run away again?"

Robyn gave me a rueful smile. "You know my brother, huh?"

"Not as well as I'd like," I muttered, and she chuckled.

"I always thought you needed your head tested liking Davy."

"I'm beginning to think you're right."

She gave me a sad smile. "He's pleased to see you, Elle. He's just scared. We don't know when the hammer is gonna fall."

I didn't pretend not to know what she meant. "The bank?"

Robyn nodded. "We just keep going, y'know?"

"What will you do?"

"We'll survive," Davy said harshly from the barn door. "Just like we always have."

He'd obviously showered and changed into a red plaid shirt, but the scowl on his face was the same. Robyn glared at her brother. He glowered right back.

I sighed inwardly and carried on brushing Raindrop. This was going to be a lot harder than I anticipated. Maybe I should have brought Lily and Greg as backup. I'd discovered why Lily had been absent from the gala and that really, was the reason I was here.

"Look," I said, drawing their attention, when it seemed as if the glare-off wasn't about to end. "I came here to talk to you both."

"I think you did your talking already," Davy snarled.

Raindrop shifted restlessly. Now it was my turn to glare at him and to my amazement he dropped his gaze. I wasn't about to have an argument around the horses. I eased out of Raindrop's stall and shut the gate.

"Night, old girl," I crooned, and she whickered in response.

"Come inside, Elle. I'll make coffee," Robyn said. "At least *I'm* interested in what you have to say." She flicked another scowl at her brother.

I brushed past Davy, feeling the same thrill I always did when I was close to him, and followed Robyn into the kitchen. I looked behind me. Davy was where I left him, so I let the screen door close on his defeated frame.

I washed up and sat at the kitchen table while Robyn made coffee in the ancient coffeemaker I remembered from before.

"So you're Elsa Ralston now?" Robyn said as she sat down.

I grimaced. "You say it like everyone else. *Elsaaa Raaaalston.*" I had never hated the sound of my name as much as I had recently.

She grinned at me. "I can say it like that if you want."

"Please don't. Just call me Elle."

Whatever Robyn was going to say was forgotten as the kitchen door opened and Davy joined us. He poured himself a coffee and sat down at the table.

He cleared his throat before he spoke. "I'm

sorry, Elle. I shouldn't be taking my anger out on you."

I nodded and smiled at him. It was a genuine apology. I knew that. Davy had never been able to fake his emotions. He wore his heart on his sleeve. Robyn was pleased too. She was just like her brother.

I stared down into my coffee. The next five minutes was either going to go well or be an utter disaster. It was fifty-fifty on the result.

"Elle?" Robyn said softly. "What's wrong?"

I looked up to see brother and sister staring at me, both looking concerned.

"I need you to listen to me, okay? Just hear me out."

Davy already looked suspicious, but Robyn nodded.

"I didn't know how the Ralston Foundation operated until a week ago." Davy's scowl deepened but I plowed on regardless. "I can't change the rules."

"Is that why you're here?" Davy asked harshly. "To crush our dreams again?"

Even Robyn looked visibly upset.

"No! No! I'm here because of this." I drew out a file and pushed it toward them. Neither of them touched it. "Please. Just look."

Robyn opened the file and read the top of the first page. "The Ralston Small Charity Foundation. You set this up?" She didn't wait for my answer as she leafed through the pages. "Wait, this mentions us."

Davy, who'd been staring at his hands, looked

up at that point. "What?"

Robyn pushed over the pages. "You want to help us rebuild the sanctuary?"

I licked my lips. "The foundation does. You'd be the first recipient. We're going to hold an auction and raise money to rebuild the sanctuary, if you'll let us."

"No." The word sounded as if it were torn from Davy's throat. "I'm not taking a cent from the Ralstons."

"Davy—" Robyn started.

Davy pushed back his chair and stormed out of the kitchen.

Robyn stood but I pushed her back down. "I'll talk to him. Why don't you read the folder? Tell me what you think."

She looked at me. "You're not playing games with us?"

I shook my head. "I'm solving a problem."

"He's going to take some persuading."

"I'll manage it," I said, hoping I sounded more confident than I felt.

I slipped on my boots and headed out after Davy. I knew where he'd go. Davy was a creature of habit. As a teenager he'd gone to the old barn when he needed a break.

Of course, I didn't realize the old barn had become the animal sanctuary, and I found him in the charred remains.

I watched him for a moment and my heart hurt at the naked pain on his face.

Oh Davy.

I kicked a stone, and it went skidding across to

where Davy stood. He stopped it with the toe of his boot.

"You always knew where to find me," he said.

"You always come to the same place," I pointed out.

He sighed, shoved his hands in his jacket and looked up at the night sky. "What do you want, Elle? My forgiveness. You've got it. You're forgiven. Now you can go back to your rich life and forget about us."

I rolled my eyes. "You always were overdramatic, Davy Jenner. You left me, remember? If anyone has the forgiving to do, it's me."

"I didn't..."

"Didn't what?" I asked.

"It doesn't matter," he said.

"You didn't dump me? Because I know you did. You walked out of my life and never returned."

I was so upset at the memory; it was hard to vocalize the words. I'd loved Davy so much and he left me like I was nothing.

He turned to face me and the pain I felt was mirrored in his expression.

"I didn't leave you, Elle. Your grandfather threatened to make the bank foreclose if I carried on seeing you. He threatened my momma and daddy, and I couldn't let that happen.

I rocked back on my heels in shock. "No."

"He did. He had the papers drawn up to throw us out. You know it was a Ralston bank."

I couldn't speak. I knew my grandfather could be a heartless man, but to do this to us, to me. I was supposed to be his favorite grandchild.

"You didn't know," Davy said.

"No." I wrapped my arms around myself, feeling as if I were going to fly apart. "He told me you were just unreliable, like all the Jenners. I thought you'd just stopped loving me. That's why I moved to Ohio. I had to get away from you."

"I never stopped loving you, Elle. Never." I could see he told the truth by the pain in his eyes, the pain that had to be mirrored in mine.

I'd always thought Davy was my soulmate. The prickly boy who became like a teddy bear around me. I never thought anything could push us apart. Then it was over just like that? The years I'd spent angry and sad at this man, and it was all down to my grandfather?

"Elle, Elle." Davy wrapped his arms around me. "Come on, breathe, honey."

I'd stopped breathing?

"Come on, just breathe. In. Out. In. Out."

I rested my head on his chest and followed his quiet instructions. My cheek rested on the soft well-washed plaid shirt, and I listened to the steady sound of his heartbeat. His arms were strong around me, holding me close. I could smell the scent of the detergent over the smell of the farm.

"You're doing good," he said, and I realized I'd been so focused on him, my breathing had settled.

I moved and Davy dropped his arms as he stepped away. I shivered at the sudden loss of his warmth.

"I'm sorry," I said. "I had no idea."

"I realize that now." He huffed. "I always knew but it was easier to blame you and your family than believe you were innocent."

"No wonder you hated the Ralstons."

"I've spent so long being angry because everything good in my life falls apart," he admitted. "You, the farm, the sanctuary, losing Momma. Nothing's ever worked out for Robyn and me."

He looked haunted and I wanted to be the one to give him comfort this time, but he took a step back, shoved his hands in his pockets and said, "I don't think I could accept help from the Ralston family."

"You're not accepting help from the Ralston family. You're accepting help from me."

"Same difference," he pointed out. "Last time I looked your name was Ralston."

I shook my head. "The name is just added to the foundation for cachet. But none of the rest of the family is involved. At the moment it's me and Lily Duchamp, and her boyfriend and his grandmother." Moonlight suddenly bathed his face and I saw his confusion. "Davy, let me talk to you and Robyn together."

I sagged, suddenly weary. I don't think I had it in me to go through this twice. I still hadn't worked out where I was eating or sleeping.

To my relief, he nodded, and we walked side by side back to the house, not speaking, but the silence wasn't uncomfortable.

The kitchen was filled with the aroma of pot roast when Davy opened the door and guided me in. Robyn was at the stove, stirring something.

She looked over and said, "Your handcuffs are in the old bunkhouse. I've given them food and blankets. I'm assuming you're staying the night?"

"I—"

"You can sleep in my room. I'll sleep in Momma's."

"What are your handcuffs?" Davy asked, bemusement written on his face.

"My protection detail." I grimaced. "I call them that for obvious reasons."

Robyn grinned at me. "They knocked on the door and asked where you were. You've been ignoring your phone. We nearly had SWAT descending on us."

Davy shook his head. "Is anyone going to explain to me why SWAT would be visiting us?"

"It's all code for calling in the police if they think I'm in danger." I pulled out my phone. Eight missed calls. No wonder they were unhappy with me. I checked my phone and realized I'd turned the sound off. "I'm going to be in so much trouble."

"They're cool. I said you were catching up on old times." Interestingly, Robyn turned pink. "The big one with the red hair, Griff, he says just message him and we'll see them in the morning."

"He did, did he?" Davy said, sounding wary.

As I sent a short and apologetic message to Griff, I wondered when my scary bodyguards turned into cool guys.

Chapter 7

Davy

I felt drained somehow, as if some of the poison which had festered inside me since the seventeen-year-old Davy was told to stay away from the girl he loved had finally drained away. Elle knew the truth now, that I'd loved her and leaving her hadn't been my idea. I hadn't intended to tell her about her grandfather. I knew how close she'd been to the old man. Better that she didn't know and kept her memories. But the rage had built up inside me and I had to let it out.

I caught the anxious glance Robyn sent my way. "I told Elle."

Elle nodded as she looked between the two of us. "I had no idea that my grandfather threatened you. I would never have let him speak to you if I'd known what he planned."

"That's what I said to Davy," Robyn said. "I told him to talk to you."

"And if I'd done that he would have hurt Momma and Daddy," I said, not hiding my bitterness. "He would have taken the farm. In the end that's gonna happen anyway. The Ralston Bank will take the farm and we'll be left with nothing. Old Man Ralston is probably laughing at us from the grave."

"Davy," Robyn chided.

The words were a lot harsher than I'd intended and I muttered an apology to Elle who just sent me a troubled glance.

"Please can we talk?" Elle said. "Please, Davy. I can help, if you'll let me."

I gave a curt nod. I knew Elle meant well but I meant what I said. I wouldn't accept a lick of help from the Ralston family, and that included Elle. I blamed them for everything that had happened to my family.

"Wash up first," Robyn ordered, sounding so like Momma it brought a lump to my throat.

I found myself next to Elle at the kitchen sink, washing our hands as we had a hundred times before as kids. She caught my gaze and we grinned at each other.

Elle must have praised Robyn for the pot roast until my sister was one huge blush.

"You do get fed by chefs now, don't you?" I asked.

"This is Momma's pot roast," Elle said indignantly, then she grinned at me, and I couldn't help returning the grin.

"It's the best," Robyn agreed. "I think Davy makes it better than me, but he always complains if he has to do the cooking."

"Just like old times," Elle agreed.

I grinned as I looked down at my empty plate. Just like old times.

"I wish Momma could have been here to see

this," Robyn said wistfully.

"Me too," Elle agreed.

I nodded, too choked up to speak. Momma would have loved to see Elle back at our kitchen table again.

But we couldn't put off the discussion any longer. With the plates cleared away and a large jug of sun tea in front of us, we sat at the table, and I prepared to listen to Elle try and convince me that this money wasn't coming from the Ralston family.

Elle took a deep breath, her long fingers on the glass of tea. She didn't even bother to look at the file and I wondered how many times she'd rehearsed the speech in her head.

"I never wanted to inherit the Ralston estate." She gave a smile that was odd, bitter even. "It was made very clear to me at the will reading that my life was over. I now belonged to Ralston, body and soul."

I winced at the thought of Elle facing the end of her life as she knew it. Elle had always been a stubborn, independent spirit. It's why old man Ralston had threatened me and my family. He'd known she would never listen to him. She would have done exactly the opposite. Now he'd gotten what he wanted. He'd finally shackled her to the family forever.

"I'm sorry, Elle," Robyn said.

Maybe it was odd, two people on the point of being made homeless feeling sorry for one of the richest women in the country. But we did, because our Elle would never have wanted this.

Still, I had to ask. "Why didn't you walk away?"

I saw the muscle twitch in her jaw. "The inheritance came with conditions."

"What kind of conditions."

"If I didn't accept, he'd bequest everything, and I mean everything, to an animal charity. The family and staff and people who worked in our businesses would be left with nothing."

Robyn's eyes were almost comically wide, and I had the feeling mine were the same.

"You're joking," I said. "The old goat."

"I wish I were. And you know what? Just for a moment, with everyone watching me, I almost told them to send it to the animals."

The irony of our circumstances wasn't lost on me.

"But you said yes," Robyn said.

Elle licked her lips as if they were suddenly dry. "No matter how much I ran away from the Ralston family, I knew they'd get me in the end. So I thought, yes, I'll take the inheritance, but I'll do things my way."

"Only to discover everyone insists on doing it the old way?" I suggested.

She inclined her head. "No one is willing to change a thing."

"Including the foundation."

"Especially the foundation," Elle said, that bitter smile back in place.

I was coming to hate that smile.

"So why are you here?" Robyn asked.

"I had a coffee with an old friend, Lily Duchamp the night after the gala. Our parents have been friends for years. She was supposed to be there, but she had a falling out with her parents. Anyway, I met her for coffee. I wanted to ask her what I could do, but I didn't even need to ask really. I noticed the difference in how the maître 'd spoke to me and how friendly he was with Lily. It turned out Lily had helped his wife raise a lot of money for her public school. A specific project for one school. With Lily's help, it saved them.

She paused to take a long gulp of tea.

I glanced up to Robyn giving me a significant look. I had no idea what it meant, but it was significant. She rolled her eyes when I returned it with a confused shrug.

Elle didn't seem to notice the exchange. She gave a little sigh. "Anyway, at the end of coffee, lunch, and more coffee, we decided to start a new foundation with the same aim in mind."

"And you thought we could be the first recipient," Robyn said.

"Yes," Elle agreed.

"You still haven't convinced me that this isn't accepting money from your family," I pointed out.

Elle furrowed her brow. "That's more difficult," she admitted.

Now it was my turn to frown. "I thought you said—" I stopped as she raised a hand.

"Let the girl speak," Robyn hissed.

I glowered at my sister, but I nodded at Elle. "I'm listening."

"I could buy your farm out and help you

rebuild the animal sanctuary without breaking a sweat," Elle pointed out.

"Isn't gonna happen," I snapped.

"Agreed," Robyn said. When we both turned to her in surprise, she shrugged. "After what your grandfather did, I wouldn't take a cent from him, even if it came from you. Sorry, Elle."

I breathed easier. My sister had my back.

Elle nodded. "Understood, and if I were in your position, I might feel the same. But, full disclosure, if you accept the money from the new foundation, you're kind of accepting a Ralston's help."

"Well, you set this up."

"Not me. The first items in the auction will be a painting by Marisa Rosen." When we both looked blank, Elle rolled her eyes. "Heathens. Long story short, Marisa paints seascapes. She has a very famous series called Lost. They were painted after her husband died. They're very sought after. Lily's boyfriend, Greg, owns three of them. Marisa is his grandmother. He's willing to add one to the auction to help you."

"I still don't see the connection with your family," Robyn said.

I was glad she asked.

"Marisa was a Ralston."

I opened my mouth to object, but Elle intervened. "A wrong side of the tracks Ralston. No money, no status. Nothing. The only reason I told you was if you found she was a Ralston and I hadn't told you, you'd go mad and do something stupid."

Robyn barked out a laugh as I glowered at Elle. "She's got you there, big brother."

I huffed, but she was right. I would have been furious if I'd discovered Marisa's name after I'd agreed.

"There's something else. Marisa hates the paintings. It reminds her of the most painful time in her life. She would like them to help fund something positive. Greg feels the same."

"And what's his family name?"

"Crenshaw. He's a gardener, more a botanist, although he calls himself a gardener."

"And he's in a relationship with Lily Duchamp?"

"Yes. They're so sweet together. They've fallen head over heels in love with each other."

That bitter smile again. It wasn't hard to work out what she was thinking. Once again, I was filled with rage at what Ralston did to us, to my Elle.

"You have a proposal in the folder?"

She nodded.

"I read it," Robyn said. "It's sound. It could work."

"Only if the bank will wait and last time I checked, they weren't in a waiting frame of mind," I pointed out.

Elle hesitated. Robyn noticed it too. She narrowed her eyes and looked at her.

"Elle?"

"You know who owns the bank?" Elle said.

We knew. We'd never gotten a choice. There wasn't a bank around these parts that wasn't owned by her family somewhere along the line.

"We know," I said, my tone grim.

"You're right. They weren't going to wait. I contacted them after the gala to find out what they were going to do."

"And?" I snarled.

Robyn laid a hand on mine, but I shook it off. "Davy, easy—"

"They would have foreclosed already," Elle said calmly.

I slumped back as if someone had punched me in the gut. Robyn gasped, a hand over her mouth.

"So why haven't they?" I demanded.

Elle hesitated again.

"Just say it, Elle. Whatever it is. What did you do?"

"I paid the mortgage arrears. It doesn't mean the farm isn't in trouble. You still owe a lot of money to a lot of people, but you're not going to be thrown out on the streets."

"You did what?"

I stared at her, mouth open, unable to believe what I'd just heard after everything I'd said to her. Robyn had her lips pressed together so tightly, they were barely visible.

"This is a stay of execution, Davy, not a gift," Elle said. "You will pay it back to me from the proceeds of the auction."

"I told you I wouldn't accept any handout from you and you said—"

"And I said you wouldn't have to, and you're not. It's a loan until the auction money comes in."

"A loan paid by a Ralston." I seethed at the betrayal.

Elle sunk her head into her hands. "What else was I meant to do, Davy?"

"It's not that we're not grateful, Elle," Robyn said, "but you have to see it from our point of view."

"Do you have the money to pay me?"

"You know we don't," I growled.

"We barely have enough money to feed ourselves," Robyn admitted.

I wanted to scowl at her for giving a Ralston that information.

"I know you don't," Elle said. "And I hate that I know, but you guys have to give me a chance to pay you back for everything you did for me when we were kids."

"What did we do?" I asked.

Her smile was shy and sweet, and I was suddenly taken back to my best friend who sat next to me, ribbing me and my sister as we ate my momma's pot roast. "You gave me a family, Davy."

Chapter 8

Elle

I helped Robyn wash up the glasses while Davy did a final check outside. Robyn was subdued and I didn't know what else to say. I had offered them the chance to save their home. If they chose not to accept it, it was up to them. At least they hadn't thrown me off the farm.

Robyn put away the last glass and dried her hands. Then she gave a sigh. "I'm sorry, Elle. We must seem very ungrateful."

"I understand why Davy hates me, but why do you?"

Robyn fixed her green gaze on me. "You hurt my brother. Well, your family did. Davy's never gotten over you, Elle. You know that. It's the Ralston name and everything it stands for."

I only heard one thing she said. Did Davy still love me? Was that true? I'd known from the first moment I saw Davy Jenner in his ill-fitting dress suit, that I'd never stopped loving the boy who walked away from me. I'd never known why he left me until today, but now I understood. It had never been Davy's choice to leave me. But could he really blame me for my grandfather's snobbery?

I put down the dishcloth and looked at Robyn. "You can hate me for my name and be homeless, or you can hate me for my name and let me make amends. But don't get me wrong. I'm not doing this to make amends for my grandfather. I am not responsible for what he did."

"Then why are you doing it?" Davy said harshly.

I turned to face him. "I should have asked you why you walked away from me. Why I was suddenly no longer welcome at the farm. Why your momma told me I couldn't come over again. I should have asked, and I didn't. And for that I'm sorry."

"That wasn't your fault," Robyn said.

"Did Momma really say you weren't welcome here," Davy asked.

"She did." I swallowed back the sudden lump in my throat. I still remembered the hurt when Momma Jenner called me and told me not to come to the farm again. Davy walked out on me and now Momma was too. It took me years to get over that. Not to feel the heartache every time someone mentioned something as simple as pot roast.

Davy walked over to me and took both my hands in his. "I'm sorry, Elle. You were the innocent in all of this, and I didn't think about you. I was so angry and scared for my momma and daddy."

I held onto his hands as tightly as I could and gazed into his green eyes. "It doesn't matter, Davy.

What matters is now. Are you going to let your pride force you out of your home? Or are you going to let me help you?"

I could see the conflict in his expression. He wanted so badly to say no to me. But he didn't let go of my hands and he didn't turn away from me.

"If Robyn agrees we'll accept the help for the animal sanctuary, and I'm going to find a way to pay you back for every cent you paid the bank." He gave me a grim smile. "Don't ask me how. I haven't worked that one out."

I let out a relieved breath and I heard Robyn do the same. We had both been scared Davy's pride would get in the way of his common sense.

"What about the rest of our debts?" Robyn asked. "Much as I hate to be the voice of doom, you were right, Elle. We have more debts than we can pay off in our lifetime. The bank was only part of it."

I turned to look at her. "Some of them can be paid off by the money from the auction. They're all tied up with the animal sanctuary. But the others are with the farm. I could pay them too and you could add it to the debt."

I saw storm clouds gathering in Davy's expression. "I want to show you something before you say no."

"I'm still gonna say no," Davy muttered.

I pulled out my phone and showed him a palomino paint horse, then I turned the phone to show Robyn.

Davy nodded curtly. "You're buying a horse? She's fine-looking. I don't understand what that has to do with us."

I smiled tenderly at the image on the screen. "Her name is Millie. She's ten years old. I rescued her. She was being abused by her previous owner. Millie is staying with a friend, but he can't take care of her long-term."

"He?" Davy asked suspiciously.

"Down, boy." I grinned at him. "You know him. Leo Harding."

Davy's expression cleared. "Oh, Robyn's boyfriend."

"He's not my boyfriend," Robyn exploded.

I chuckled. "Not for want of trying. Does he still send you bluebonnets?"

Robyn groaned and buried her head in her hands.

Davy and I smirked at each other. Leo's teenage crush on Robyn had been a source of amusement because of the flowers he sent her, not realizing she suffered dreadful allergies. His feelings had never been reciprocated. Leo and I had remained friends and fortunately he'd found a wonderful woman who did appreciate the flowers. But he'd obviously be forever Robyn's boyfriend in the Jenner household.

"Leo and Charlie are moving across state to a smaller place. I could bring Millie home, but I don't have time to take care of her. She needs someone who's experienced with horses." I hadn't thought of it before, but it would solve my problem and could take care of another one. "If you boarded Millie until she was well, we could work out a price and take that off the debt. She needs a sanctuary. But more than that, she needs a home. Just like I did."

Davy rolled his eyes. "You know how to turn the screw, don't you?"

I gave him my best wide-eyed look. "I don't know what you mean."

"Elle, that look didn't work when I was fifteen and it won't work now."

"But Elle is right," Robyn said. "You're the best person I know to take care of an abused horse. She has to come here."

Davy looked between me and his sister. "I'm not gonna have a choice, am I?"

"No!" we said in unison.

I sobered rapidly. "She's not an easy horse to take care of, Davy. She doesn't trust anyone. Not even Leo or me." I scrolled through my phone and showed him the photos of Millie as I found her. He paled and showed the screen to Robyn.

"She's a million times better than when I rescued her, but the scars run deep."

"Millie's coming here," Robyn stated. Both Davy and I knew there was no room for negotiation.

"I'll pay your debts in return for her board. You and Robyn can work out a price and Robyn can set up an account. If you need an extra hand, I can organize that too. I had to do that for Leo. Millie takes time, Davy. All I ask is you give her a chance. There's one more thing. Don't let anyone ride her. She won't take that."

Davy folded his arms across his chest and glowered at me. "For a Ralston who didn't want to be a Ralston, you're doing a good impression of one."

"Maybe. But I'm a Ralston who cares—cared—for you. Don't you forget that." And if that was a bit fierce there was a reason for it.

There was a sharp rap at the kitchen door. Before Davy or I could move, Robyn opened the door.

I wasn't surprised to see one of my handcuffs, Griff, standing there. I was surprised to see Robyn fluttering over him.

"Jamie heard raised voices earlier. I'm just checking you're all right."

It amused me to note that although the question was obviously aimed at me, Griff's ice-blue eyed attention was focused on Robyn.

I left Robyn to assure my big scary bodyguard that everything was all right. Davy and I leaned against the kitchen cabinets to watch this play out. Davy leaned against me, and I rested my head against his shoulder. Griff didn't notice but from the way Davy stiffened, then relaxed, he definitely did and he didn't move away from me.

"I've never seen my sister so interested in a guy," Davy murmured. "Did he have to have red hair?"

"I've never seen my bodyguard forget I was alive," I whispered. "Can I take blackmail photos?"

"Not if you want to live," Griff said without looking my way.

I pouted but inwardly I was cracking up. Griff wasn't going to live this down in a hurry. I also wouldn't tell my mother. She wouldn't approve.

I thanked Robyn for letting me sleep in her bed and retired for the night, exhausted and somewhat relieved that I was still here and not on my way back to Boston, my tail between my legs.

Davy wasn't happy with what I had to say, but he was listening to me, and that was the main thing. I wanted to help him and Robyn and if I had to batter their doors down to let me do it, I would do. I'm not sure where feisty Elle came from, but I was liking the new me.

I sat on the bed and looked around Robyn's bedroom. Not much had changed since I was last here. The schoolbooks were gone and in their place were an array of novels, but I could close my eyes and pretend I was seventeen again and sleeping over.

The knock on the door made me jump.

"Yes?"

"It's Davy. May I come in?"

"Yes, of course." My voice cracked a little.

The door opened and Davy came in, still fully dressed. He smiled at me, somewhat sheepishly.

"Can we talk?" he asked.

I felt as if I'd done nothing *but* talk, but I nodded and patted the bed next to me.

Davy sat down with a sigh. "Elle, I'm sorry. I know I've not treated you right since the gala. You have to understand, it's not you."

Unfortunately, I understood only too well. "It's the Ralston name."

"Yes."

"I've already had this conversation with

Robyn."

Davy's lips twitched. "Typical of Robyn. She always has to get here first."

"She always did. But at least she tried to make me understand what was going on."

"Robyn always has my back. Even when I don't deserve it," he admitted.

"I want to have your back too, Davy," I said. "I want you to understand you're not on your own."

Davy sighed again and took my hand. "Elle, please will you help me save Black Feather farm?"

"Yes, Davy."

I breathed a sigh of relief. He would let me help him.

There was a long silence.

"You paid those debts off already, didn't you?"

I hadn't expected to be caught out so quickly. "I did. How did you find out?"

"I received a call from Millers Feed. Miller said he'd be delivering an order in the morning now we were up to date. And to thank young Miss Elle for calling him direct. His wife was thrilled to talk to her again." He sighed. "You know I should be shouting at you now."

"Could you wait 'til morning, Davy?" I yawned and leaned against him. "I'm too tired to think straight now."

He pressed a kiss to my palm. "Your hands are a little rough."

I grimaced. "From the gardening business. That's why they make me wear gloves."

"It makes you more real somehow." He sounded almost wondering. Then he kissed my temple and stood. "G'night, Elle."

"Night, Davy."

"It's good to see you here again," he said softly and left the room.

"It's good to be here," I said to the empty room and meant it.

Chapter 9

Davy

Sleep evaded me for the night, and I spent the hours sitting on the window ledge, watching the moon move through the star-lit sky. My mind was too busy thinking of the woman sleeping in my sister's bedroom. I couldn't believe Elle—she would always be my Elle—was sleeping not ten feet from me just like she used to.

I worked through a myriad of emotions. Shock at seeing Elle. Anger. Yes, I had to acknowledge the anger at her highhanded approach, even as I was so grateful for a reprieve on keeping our home. So gratitude and pride. My pride which had taken a knock, and pride at what a woman Elle had become.

The gawky ginger-haired teenager had become a titian-haired beauty. I once heard my momma describe Robyn like that. I guess it was true for all three of us. I wish I'd seen Elle's metamorphosis. I was still angry that was taken away from me. But I knew I couldn't hold onto the anger forever. Robyn was always telling me it was toxic to hold grudges. When did my little sister get so wise?

I needed to put that anger toward her family behind me and focus on the woman Elle had become. Kind of heart, generous of spirit, a true beauty inside and out. She had looked at our circumstances and worked through to find a solution. What did she see when she looked at me? It wasn't hard to imagine. An angry bitter cowboy, full of his own pride and arrogance. I was ashamed that I'd become so bitter and twisted.

I stared out of the window. Somewhere in the darkness of my farm was the phoenix of the animal sanctuary waiting to rise again. We could do this. It wasn't going to make us money. The animal sanctuary had been my mother's dream, running alongside the farm. It was time I faced up to the fact I would never be the farmer my daddy was. Was there something else I could do to bring income into Black Feather farm? It was time I asked people for help. Since Momma died, I'd been pushing her friends away. My daddy's friends too. Good people with a wealth of experience of working this land.

"You've been a stubborn fool, Davy Jenner," I said out loud.

It wasn't easy to acknowledge it but it had to be said.

The clock ticked around minute by minute. Sleep was still a distant memory. I pulled out my little used laptop, logged in hoping that I didn't have to remember my passwords, and did some research. Once I clicked on Marisa Rosen, I realized just how much money would be coming our way. The paintings from the Lost collection were worth millions. Even one painting would be more than enough to secure our future for a while. Marisa had been a Ralston but she'd turned her back on that name years before. And her grandson had offered his help as manual labor. I read about him too. At least he knew what he was doing with power tools.

I'd be a fool to turn down these kind folks' help.

As dawn approached, I made a decision. I dressed quickly in my plaid shirt and Wranglers, then I left my bedroom and gently knocked on the door opposite me. I waited, but all I heard was silence broken by a distant bleat of a sheep. I turned away and then the door opened, and Elle blinked at me sleepily.

"Davy, is everything all right?"

"Would you come watch the sunrise with me?"

"Over Feather Creek?" Even in the darkness I could tell she was smiling.

"Yes."

Elle and I, and Robyn if she could be bothered to get up, spent our teenage years riding out to watch the sunrise at Feather Creek.

"I'd love to," she said. "Are we riding? Could I borrow something from Robyn to wear?"

"Take a look in her closet," I said, generously gifting my sister's clothes.

"I'll be five minutes."

"Great. Meet you in the kitchen."

"There'd better be coffee," she said.

I made a scoffing noise. "There's always coffee."

I jogged down the stairs as she closed the bedroom. I knew I had this big goofy grin on my face. The cute girl wanted to watch the sunrise with me.

I had just enough time to make coffee before she joined me. I poured the dark brew into two travel mugs.

Elle was in the kitchen in exactly five minutes, dressed in a faded plaid shirt and jeans. She looked more like my Elle than the socialite from yesterday. It made me relax. She still looked sleepy, but she wore the same goofy smile that was on my face.

"Creamer?" I asked, handing her a cup.

"I think I'd better drink it neat if I'm going to stay awake." She took a sip from the travel mug and coughed. "I can tell you made the coffee."

"Strong enough to put hairs on your chest Momma used to say."

"I don't want hairs on my chest, thank you very much," she said tartly, then grinned at me.

I knew there was no way she was going to stop drinking the coffee, no matter how strong it was.

"Robyn has a spare pair of boots in the hall closet."

"I always used to borrow her clothes when I was here before," Elle murmured. "She used to keep a pile in the corner of her closet. I went into her closet and they're still there. Lucky I'm still the same size."

I stared at her. "I had no idea she did that."

It reminded me that I wasn't the only person who lost Elle. My sister had lost her best friend too. Maybe we'd both found it hard to move on. She was just better hiding it than I was.

We took our coffee out to the barn and drank it

as we saddled up the horses. Maybe it was too cold to be doing this, but I wasn't going to miss the chance of seeing another sunrise with Elle Ralston.

"You take Raindrop and I'll ride Lemondrop," I suggested.

We only had two horses left now. Raindrop and Robyn's old mare, Lemondrop. I'd had to sell the younger horses, some of them I'd raised from foals and were family to me.

Raindrop was my horse. I'd raised her from a foal too. But Elle had always loved her.

Her smile lit up the dim light in the barn. "Hear that, Raindrop. I get to ride you today."

The mare nickered as if she approved.

"She's supposed to love me best," I said, mournfully.

Raindrop tossed her head and we both laughed. My horse always knew how to put me in my place.

We could have watched the sunrise from the comfort of the verandah, but as kids we liked getting away from the parents. I still preferred to watch the sunrise at the creek and wallow in my memories. We rode out, the cold taking our breath away, our breaths just visible in the early light.

Elle rode with the same ease and grace she'd always had, smiling over at me like a little kid in a candy store. "I never thought I'd see Feather Creek again."

"You couldn't stay here and not go to Feather Creek."

"Do you still ride?"

Elle wrinkled her nose. "Not since I left here. I

spent too much time trying to build up my business. Not much call for horses in landscape gardening." She studied me. "You look tired. Did you sleep at all last night?"

"No," I admitted honestly. "I had too much to think about. Sorry if I woke you up."

"It's okay. I can sleep any time. I was usually up early with my business."

"What made you decide to do landscape gardening?" I asked.

She grinned at me. "I love gardening. You remember that? I was always digging your momma's yard. And it really annoyed my mother."

There was so much I could say to that, but for once I took the diplomatic route and kept my mouth shut. Her mom wasn't so keen on me. We weren't good enough for her daughter. I'd always gotten along with her dad and he and my daddy had been fishing buddies until *his* father broke my heart. After that, my daddy had put away his fishing rods and as far as I know never fished again. Yet another Jenner hurt by the Ralston patriarch. I wondered if her father had missed his fishing buddy.

"What did she want you to do?" I asked.

"Before she knew my grandfather's plans, she had ideas of me becoming a model. She had visions watching me treading the catwalks in Paris and Milan."

I smirked at her disgusted expression, and she gave a reluctant laugh. Elle would have loathed anything to do with fashion, preferring to be up to her elbows in dirt.

"You know me too well," she said ruefully.

Once upon a time I did, but maybe Elle was still my Elle. My Elle. Now there was a dangerous path I didn't want to go down. My heart wouldn't take it for a second time.

"Nearly there," I said, more to distract myself than to let her know. Elle knew our farm almost as well as I did.

Elle's face lit up; her excitement obvious. "I can't wait."

There had been enough rainfall in the past month that there was water in the creek, although in summer it was usually dry, and the only danger was an unexpected gulley washer.

We reached the creek, sliding off the horses and ground-tied them. Then we stood in our favorite spot waiting for the sun to show its first rays. We stood side by side as the sky started to show the first streaks of pinks and mauves.

Elle let out a huge sigh. "I've come home," she murmured.

"Elle."

She turned to me, and her expression seemed to be hopeful. "Yes?"

"This is your home. Whenever you want. I know you're like stupidly rich and probably have homes all over the world, but don't stay away. You know Robyn and I lo...want you here." I stumbled over the words, but Elle's sweet smile made my heart miss a beat.

"Thanks, Davy. I have no idea where my home is now, but you...Black Feather farm is more home to me than anywhere else I've lived."

I hated the way we danced around each other when we both seemed to have so much to say. Our gazes locked and the need to take her in my arms and kiss her was overwhelming. I almost took that step when she turned back to look at the sunrise.

"Oh Davy. Look at the sky. I'd almost forgotten the colors."

Reluctantly, I dragged my gaze away from her. It was beautiful. Deep blues and pinks and purples. With the faintest glow of the orange sun just starting to peep above the horizon. I saw the sunrise every day, but it was never as special as when Elle was by my side.

I took a chance and put my arm around her shoulders casually, ready to pull away if she stiffened. But Elle made a small happy sound and nestled into me, her arm going around my waist. I gave up any pretense this was just a casual hug and wrapped my other arm around her. My girl was in my arms once more. I pressed the lightest of kisses to the top of her head, inhaling the light floral scent of her bright hair. This moment was the happiest I'd been in ten years. How could I let her go?

Chapter 10

Elle

As I nestled in the security of Davy's strong arms, I watched the sun rise slowly into a glowing orange globe in the deep blue sky. I couldn't believe he was holding me again as he used to when we were sixteen. We were kids then although we didn't think we were. We thought we were going to spend the rest of our lives as Mr. and Mrs. Jenner, make red-haired babies, and work the farm together. We had such expectation. We spent hours in this exact spot, discussing our life together as we watched the sun rise on another day. We were so naïve in our joyful plans.

A decade later, I was in the arms of a man, not a boy. This man had been hardened by long hours working the land, but also by his grief at everything he'd lost. And I was the cause of it. At least my family was. But surely this morning proved Davy wasn't lost to me? He'd had been so angry last night, I thought he was unreachable, that he'd throw me out before we had a chance to talk. But this morning he woke me up to see the sunrise.

I leaned back against Davy, knowing I had to go home today, and wishing desperately I could stay and watch a lifetime of sunrises together. He said this could be my home too but what was he really offering me? A place to land occasionally or a lifetime in his arms?

"I wish you'd stay," Davy whispered.

It was as if he read my thoughts.

I tilted my head to look at him. "I wish I could."

He looked resigned. "I know. You've got another life to lead."

A life that would help others but that seemed so empty without him.

"I'll come back," I promised.

He held onto me a little tighter before letting me go with a sigh. I missed his arms around me.

"So what happens next? I know you've got the auction to organize," he asked.

And now we were back to business. I tried to formulate my thoughts so I could give him the information he needed.

He and Robyn had agreed to the auction, so I'd done what I set out to do here. He'd even coped with me clearing all the farm's debts. I'd taken care of more than that, but I hope that didn't come back to bite me later. I didn't want to overwhelm him at this stage.

"I need as much information from you and Robyn so I can sell this to our patrons."

"Robyn is better at that than I am," Davy admitted.

"I know. But I need you and Robyn at the auction."

Davy shook his head. "No. Once was enough."

"It's non-negotiable, Davy. They want to see

what they're paying for."

His scowl deepened. "I've done this already. I'm not being trussed up like a turkey again."

I beamed at him for unwittingly echoing my words. "If I can't wear my boots, you can't wear your Wranglers."

"What?" Now he just looked confused.

I explained the conversation I'd had with my mother the night of the foundation dinner, and his expression cleared.

"I'd have given anything to see you wear that dress and jewels, and your work boots. It might have made me less out of place."

I gave an indelicate snort. "Mom would never have allowed me out if I'd been dressed like that."

"Next time bring your boots."

I gave Davy a mock salute. "Yessir!"

We grinned at each other again, then Davy grimaced. "I don't think we could afford to get to Boston again."

I knew how much that admission must have cost him.

"The small charity foundation will handle your flights and what you both wear," I said smoothly. "You'll stay with me, so you won't have to worry about a hotel."

He nodded as he thought about it, then he scowled at me. "Is it always gonna be like this, Mizz Elsa. You telling me what to do and me saying yes, ma'am, no ma'am?"

I gave him another bright smile. "It always was like this, Davy. You just don't remember."

He grunted and I giggled.

"Even if you've paid the creditors I can't last much longer," he said. "We're making no money on the farm and Robyn is having to take in extra accounts work to put food on the table.

Another painful admission which seemed to be dragged up from his soul.

"Davy, can we ride back to the stables? I've got an idea."

He huffed. "How many more horses have you rescued?"

"Just the one...so far."

"It's going to be an alpaca or a llama, isn't it?" Davy grumbled.

I blinked. "What? I'm confused."

"You're going to ask me to rescue an alpaca or a llama."

"Davy, I've got no idea what you're talking about. I was going to suggest taking care of horses. But if you want camels then I'm sure we can—"

"Llamas, not camels," he corrected.

Davy Jenner was a weird man, there was no doubt about it.

Davy stared at me, the horror clear on his face. Robyn wore much the same expression.

We sat with the remains of breakfast in front of us and tall glasses of sun tea. It had taken me that long to work up my courage to make my suggestion.

"No way," he spat.

"Why not? You don't have to do it all the time and it would be money coming onto the ranch."

"Black Feather farm is a working farm, not a

dude ranch."

"But it's not working, is it?" I said gently. "The farm's been losing money since your dad was alive." I hated the twin looks of betrayal facing me but there wasn't time to be gentle now. They were at crisis point.

"We're not a ranch," Davy pointed out, his face pinched. "The two of us can't manage the farm, the animal sanctuary, and catering for city folk too."

"Where would they sleep?" Robyn asked.

"What about the bunkhouse?" I suggested. "That's been unused since you let the hands go."

"Your security may deal with it, but it's not in a fit state for fine folk to sleep in. Even the hands complained about it."

Davy exhaled a long breath. "I know what you're trying to do, Elle, and thank you. But Robyn and I are beaten down. We can only deal with one thing at a time."

Robyn nodded. "If we had any sense, we'd walk away from the farm and give the bank the keys. They could turn it into a golf course."

I saw Davy flinch and turn away from his sister. I guessed this was a conversation they'd had more than once.

I focused on Robyn. I remember her as a ten-year-old, telling me she was going to go to college and become a lawyer. I remember the indulgent, yet sad, expressions of her parents. They had known there would be no money for college, let alone law school. "What do *you* want to do? You used to want to go to college."

"That dream faded a long time ago. I knew I'd never get away from the farm." Robyn grimaced. "I'm sorry, Davy."

Davy reached out and squeezed his sister's hand. "It's okay. I never wanted to leave the farm. You never had a choice."

I ached for my friends. If they'd let me, I could make both their dreams come true, yet I knew they'd turn me down flat.

"Davy's right," I said, and their attention turned to me. "You need to deal with one thing at a time. Let me ask you a question, and I need an honest answer from both of you. Do you want the animal sanctuary?"

Both siblings smiled at me and something inside me relaxed.

"We do," Robyn said.

"Then the auction goes ahead. And you're both coming."

I ignored their twin groans. "It's one night and your chance to shine. You won't be competing against anyone else this time. You guys are the star attraction."

"I'm not wearing another tux," Davy stated flatly.

I chewed on my bottom lip and studied him for a long time. "Maybe you don't have to."

He gave me a suspicious glower. "I don't trust that look."

"Do you trust me?"

Davy hesitated and I understood. Of course he didn't trust me, and that hurt. But he wanted to. I could see that too.

I leaned forward and patted his hand. "No tuxedo. And you can wear jeans. But let me organize that."

"Do I still get a pretty dress?" Robyn asked anxiously.

I grinned at her. "Yes, if you want one."

"This will be my one and only chance to get a dress made for me. Of course I want one," she declared, "but maybe not the heels."

I breathed a sigh of relief that I had only one temperamental Jenner to clothe. "Then we'll talk to my dressmaker, Valerie. She's Greg's sister, Lily Duchamp's boyfriend."

Robyn wrinkled her brow. "Do you all know each other?"

"Not me. I'm new in town, remember. But Lily has connections with everyone."

"I can't wait to see you feeding the chickens in a designer dress," Davy muttered.

Robyn thumped his arm. I thought it was deserved and cackled at them both.

The knock at the door, although not unexpected, made me sigh. It was time to go back to reality. I smiled at Griff who nodded at me. It didn't escape my attention the way his eyes flickered to Robyn, or the way the color heightened in her cheeks.

"Time to go?" I asked.

"We'll need to leave in thirty minutes," he said.

The door closed again, and we were all silent. Then Davy glanced at me. "If you're packed, we could take a walk."

It was my turn to pink a little. "I just need to

change but I'd like to walk with you first."

He smiled, obviously relieved.

Robyn flapped her hands at us, making a shooing motion. "Go on then."

"You know she just wants to talk to Griff, don't you?" I said as we strolled across the yard.

"Of course I do," Davy muttered. "She coulda picked a guy closer to home."

I snorted.

He stared at me, then rolled his eyes. "I guess that was a stupid thing to say."

"You know Griff goes everywhere I go," I pointed out. "We'll always be double-dating."

The look of horror on his face was so worth the shove I received.

"You don't want to double-date?" I asked, all faux innocence.

"My sister is never going to date," Davy declared.

I kept quiet. I knew about Robyn's high school crush on Henry Miller even if Davy didn't. I'd looked through her yearbook last night and found the hearts by his name.

Davy gave me a shy smile that made my heart flutter and held out his hand. I forgot all about Henry Miller.

"Let's visit with the horses," he said.

I took his hand and walked with him to the paddock where we'd turned the two horses out after our dawn ride. They lipped lazily at the grass, paying little attention to us. I rested my arms on the fences and watched them, more content in that moment than I'd been for a long time.

Despite his prickliness, I had always been happy in Davy's company. Now I was going to have to go back to Boston and leave him behind. I didn't like the thought of that at all. I took a risk and glanced at him. To my surprise he was watching me intently.

Davy laid a hand over mine. "It'll be all right, Elle."

I wasn't sure what he was talking about. The animal sanctuary or the farm or the two of us. I really hoped he included us in that.

Davy sighed and turned to look at the horses, but he left his hand where it was.

Chapter 11

Davy

Letting Elle leave was going to be hard. For the first time since the day I'd walked away from her, I'd been happy. She made me happy. How was I going to keep her? I had nothing to offer. Elle had the world. But I had a feeling she felt the same sense of insecurity as she had a death grip on my hand.

I would find a way to keep her in my life, even if it was only friendship that I could offer her. I had a feeling Elle needed friends.

Elle stopped in her tracks, tugging me into the shadows as we entered the small yard.

"Uh, why are we lurking here?" I asked.

"Is that your sister kissing my bodyguard?"

I followed her gaze and frowned at the sight. "I think it's *your* bodyguard kissing *my* sister."

Robyn was on the stoop, a few steps up. Griff was kissing her, his hands cupping her jaw. Neither of them spotted us, too lost in each other.

"I think you're right," Elle murmured.

I pressed my lips together. I wanted my sister to be happy, but I didn't want some fly-by-night bodyguard coming in and playing with her affections. She wasn't experienced where men were concerned. Neither of us had that much experience I had to admit.

I deliberately kicked a stone across the yard, and they looked up. Robyn gave me a guilty look. Griff did much the same to Robyn, which was kind of amusing. I guess he was on the clock.

"Elsa—" he started, but she shook her head.

"It's okay, Griff. Sorry to have interrupted you guys."

Griff went so red he almost matched his hair. I had been there so many times. Griff flicked a glance at me. I gave him a cool look. He could probably kill me with one finger, but if he hurt my kid sister, I'd take him down. Griff gave me a nod as if he followed my thoughts. Then he looked at Elle. I gave him the nod. We understood each other.

"I need to get my bags." Elle left my side and scurried into the house.

"I'll help you," Robyn said hastily, following Elle.

Well, that was subtle.

When the screen door shut behind them, Griff turned to me. "I like Robyn."

I folded my arms across my chest and surveyed him coolly. "I can see that."

"Would you object to me courting your sister?"

Courting. Such an old-fashioned word. But somehow I appreciated the formality, so I was honest with him. "No, I don't mind, if you treat her right." I let the threat hang there.

Griff gave me the courtesy of not laughing in my face. "I will."

"But it's not like you'll see her that much," I pointed out. "I thought where Elle—Elsa—went, so did you."

"I kinda got the impression she'll be back here on a frequent basis." He saw my look of surprise and groaned. "This isn't a discussion she's had with you?"

"Not yet," I murmured, although it gave me a warm feeling in the pit of my belly.

Griff rolled his eyes. "She's planning to come back, man."

I couldn't hold back the smile. Elle would be coming back to me.

"You guys should really talk to each other," he said.

"Like you and Robyn were?"

He blushed again. He must have hated that as a kid. I know I did. Before either of us could say anything else, Elle returned in the clothes she'd arrived in. I missed *my* Elle.

"I'm ready," she said to Griff.

He nodded and disappeared inside the bunkhouse to collect the others.

Elle turned to me. She wore a pensive expression I didn't quite understand. "Back to reality."

"*This* is reality," I told her. "Your life is a fantasy."

"It's not my fantasy." Now she looked sad.

I ran a finger down her cheek. "Come back to me, Elle."

"I will. The auction—"

"No. Leave Boston and live with us here."

I could see the longing in her eyes. Elle didn't want to leave. This was where she belonged. But I saw the longing replaced with regret, and she straightened her shoulders. In that moment I saw old man Ralston in here as she went from Elle to Elsa. Whatever happened between us, she could never live here.

"I have to go," she said. "It's my role now. I can't let my family down."

I gave the lightest brush of my thumb over her lips and stepped back. "I know you can't, and nor can I."

Our gazes locked, then she looked away as Griff and the other security detail exited the bunkhouse. There was no sign of Robyn.

Elle sighed. "I'll call you regarding the auction. Don't yell at me." She nodded at Griff and headed to the large SUV.

It took me a moment for my brain to catch up. "What have you done?" I demanded.

But the doors were closed, and the SUV pounded down the road to the highway, clouds of dust obscuring my view.

"What have you done?" I said to the empty yard.

And where was Robyn?

I jogged up the stoop and into the kitchen. "Hey, Robyn. Where are you?"

"In the office."

"You didn't want to say goodbye to your boyfriend?" I asked as I walked in. She turned to me, her face pale. "What's wrong?" I demanded, seriously worried now. "What did he do to you?" If

I had to get my shotgun and chase after them I would.

"The bank just called. I had to speak to them. That's why I didn't come out."

I grimaced. "Are they chasing for the next instalment already? I thought they'd give us breathing space."

Robyn shook her head. "She's paid the mortgage."

I stared at her. "What?"

"The farm is ours, Davy. Elle paid off the mortgage."

"She did what?"

"She paid off the mortgage." Robyn repeated it for the third time as if I were a child needing a patient explanation.

I pulled my cell phone out of my pocket.

"Don't do anything stupid, Davy. She did this because she loves you. Don't make her change her mind."

I clenched my jaw, my hands flexing as if they wanted to punch something. They did. I did. "I told her I didn't want to be in debt to a Ralston."

"You accepted her paying the arrears."

"And the local stores," I admitted.

"All our debts combined was less than the value of those sapphires she wore. This is pocket change to Elle." Robyn spoke urgently and she didn't take her gaze off me. She was genuinely worried what I was about to do next.

"She ignored everything I said," I muttered.

"She'd already paid it off before she arrived," Robyn said. "Elle could hardly go ask for her money back."

I folded my arms across my chest and glowered at my sister. "She should have told us."

"Yes, she should. But you know why she didn't."

As I slumped into the office chair. Robyn threaded her fingers through my hair. "Let it go, Davy. We've got a chance to make the animal sanctuary that Momma wanted. Let's not waste that opportunity."

"I wish—"

"Me too."

She hugged me close, and I rested my head against her.

"So I shouldn't go yelling at her then?" I muttered.

"Not today. She did something good even if she can't understand why you hate it so much."

"It still sticks in my craw."

"Me too," she admitted.

"And we're never gonna be able to pay her back."

"I've been thinking about that."

I looked up at the sudden determined note in my sister's voice. "Oh?"

"You know how miserable she looks every time she talks about her new life? And how happy she looks when she's here?"

I nodded. It hadn't been hard to miss.

"Then we offer her sanctuary," Robyn said. "Somewhere she can come when she needs a break. Black Feather farm can be her home too."

"Do you think she needs a rundown old farm as

a sanctuary when she could go to anywhere in the world?" I scoffed.

Robyn frowned at me. "Davy, this is home to Elle. This rundown old farm is all she's ever thought of as home."

"What about Ohio?"

"That was just somewhere to escape to," she pointed out. "Somewhere you weren't. When you dumped her, she lost her safe place."

"I didn't dump her," I muttered. "I was told to stay away."

Robyn held me tighter. "And now you have a chance to change that. She's begging you to give her that chance. She could have picked any one of a thousand charities to start this new foundation. But she picked us. She chose you. Don't you wreck it for us, Davy Jenner. And by us, I mean you, me, Elle..."

"And Griff?" I teased as she trailed away.

"I really like him," Robyn admitted. "But if Elle doesn't come back here, neither will he. Griff said as much."

I huffed. "He can get on a plane, can't he?"

"The Ralstons keep him running over the world. He showed me his schedule. It's booked out for the next eighteen months."

"Which means Elle's schedule is too," I said, not liking that idea at all, but also realizing Elle made time to create the new charitable foundation and come here.

"She cancelled events to come here," Robyn said as if she'd read my mind. "She's gonna be working twice as hard to catch up."

I felt ashamed. I'd gotten the idea her role was just a cosmetic one. A pretty face on the Ralston website. I didn't realize how much work was involved. I stood and rolled my shoulders. "I need a coffee. We need to decide what to do next."

"We?" Robyn eyed me suspiciously.

"We," I agreed. "I'm still not happy about being beholden to any Ralston, but Elle did it for us. All of us."

I wasn't happy, and Elle and I would have to work through that, but no one else could have saved us at that point. And as Robyn had pointed out, it was more than about my pride. Elle didn't want to lose the only home she'd cared about, and Robyn didn't want to lose the chance of love. As for me, I wanted Elle in my arms again.

The coffee was hot, strong, and sustained Robyn and me through a long and difficult discussion. At this point, with no debt hanging over us, we could sell up and walk away, with no need for the auction. We would have enough money for Robyn to go to school—she was clever enough to walk into any college—and me to retrain as something else. I didn't have the smarts, but I'd thought about something practical like carpentry or plumbing. The animal sanctuary had been my momma's dream. We could walk away now.

I put this to Robyn, trying to frame it as the big opportunity it was. I would never stand in the way of my sister's dreams. But her face twisted.

"I can't bear the thought of leaving the farm," she murmured.

"Robyn, this is our chance for something new. You don't have to be stuck here. You could go into the world and fulfil your dreams."

She glared at me across the table. "And what about you? All you've sacrificed, Davy."

"What have I sacrificed," I scoffed.

Robyn leaned over and squeezed my hand. "You lost Elle."

I sighed. "That was a long time ago. Now we've gotten new opportunities and we shouldn't waste them."

"I want to see the animal sanctuary open," Robyn insisted. "I can take courses online, but we never had the money before."

Her hesitation made me narrow my eyes. We didn't have the money *now* unless we sold the farm. The answer wasn't hard to look for.

"Elle offered to pay your college tuition?" I said.

"She said she would help me. There are education grants she would help me with. I said I wouldn't do anything until I'd discussed it with you."

I loved my sister. If I stood in her way, would she ever forgive me? She wasn't the one who had an issue with the Ralston family.

"You should get your degree," I said firmly. "We'll make it work."

"I'm staying here. We have so much work to get the animal sanctuary rebuilt and open."

Robyn was just as firm. I knew there was no point arguing with her. But Elle? I was brewing for a nice little fight with her.

Chapter 12

Elle

So maybe I left a bomb waiting to explode behind me and ran. I knew that was cowardly of me. But I also knew that if I stayed and Davy found out what I'd done, the fallout wouldn't be pretty.

I stared out the window, my attention never leaving the farm until we reached the highway. Despite knowing how angry Davy was going to be when he found out I'd paid off the mortgage, the urge to tell the driver to turn around and leave me there was overwhelming. I caught Griff's miserable expression. He'd stared out of the back window since we left the yard.

"We'll return soon," I promised. We were alone in the back, so I wasn't betraying any secrets in front of his team. "You'll see her soon."

He sighed and forced a smile on his face. "I know. It's been a long time since I met anyone. Not since my wife left, you know?"

I knew Griff had been divorced for about five years. His wife couldn't handle the long separations when he was on assignments. She'd divorced him and married a grade schoolteacher. Griff was happy for her, but I knew he was lonely.

We spent a lot of time traveling together and talking about our lives. I had told him about Black Feather farm and the Jenner family before Davy and Robyn made a reappearance in my life. And now he'd fallen for Robyn Jenner. How would that play out, I wondered. Davy would hate it if Griff broke Robyn's heart.

"Don't break Robyn's heart," I warned.

Griff glowered at me. "I've already had the big brother speech. I don't need the big sister speech too. Besides, we need to talk about you ignoring your phone calls. We were on the point of pushing the emergency button."

"I'm sorry," I said, trying to sound sincere. It obviously didn't work because his frown deepened. I huffed. "I got...involved. It always happens around Davy Jenner."

Griff's lips twitched and his scowl eased a fraction. "He seems kind of intense."

"He always was," I sighed. That was one of the things I'd loved about him.

"And angry," Griff suggested.

"And that." I'd always been able to smooth away Davy's anger with a hug and a kiss.

"He's not going to be happy when he discovers what you did."

"No," I agreed. "But it had to be done. There was no other way."

"So it was worth sacrificing his pride?"

I wasn't sure if Griff approved or not.

"To keep them in their home? I think it was worth it, and I hope Davy will see that once he's calmed down."

"And if he doesn't?" Griff asked.

I stared at him. "They've gotten options for the first time in their lives, Griff. They can stay or sell up. The Jenners have never had options. I love that farm. It's the one place I called home. The last thing I want is for them to sell, but it's been a noose around their necks. I won't stand in their way if they do."

"And what happens if they decide to sell?" Griff asked.

"Then we don't need the auction. Or maybe we'll find another nonprofit which needs help now."

"What do you think they'll do?"

I stared out of the window at a passing gas station. "I think they'll stay. Their love for their momma will make them see it through. And the Jenner stubbornness."

"I'd like to help them rebuild the animal sanctuary," Griff said. He gave a wry smile. "The bunkhouse could use some work too."

I studied him for a moment, then nodded. "You can take a leave of absence if you want to help them. Paid, of course. You'll be helping the charity, so I'll make sure your wages are covered."

Griff blinked. "Are you sure you're a Ralston?" Then he apologized.

I snorted. My family's reputation was in the dumpster. "Don't worry. We'll wait to see what Davy—David and Robyn decide to do first."

"How long do you think it will be before Mr. Jenner finds out you paid off his mortgage."

I looked at my watch. "About fifteen minutes

ago. The bank called just before we left. That's why Robyn didn't come outside to say goodbye. She's not stupid. She'll wait before she tells him."

"She's good at manipulation too?" Griff didn't sound that impressed.

I frowned, not liking the way he talked about Robyn or me. "Robyn wants what's best for Davy. She loves her brother. She also knows that sometimes he can't see the wood for the trees."

"A man has his pride," he pointed out.

"He does," I agreed, "and pride comes before a fall. But in this case, pride would have made them homeless. This way they have a breathing space to decide what to do without wondering if the bailiffs are going to arrive on the doorstep. He can pay me back every cent when he sells the farm if that makes him happier."

"Do you think he will?"

"Yes." I smiled at the burly bodyguard. "He's like you. He won't accept any man's help without knowing how to return it."

"I don't know what you mean," Griff spluttered.

My smile changed into a smirk. "I think you do."

After his divorce, Griff hit rock bottom and the bottle, and was on the point of being fired from the firm that handled my family's security, when my grandfather decided to try a different approach. He liked Griff and didn't want to lose him. He insisted Griff went into rehab and thankfully, Griff accepted the help and turned his life around. Since then, he'd been wholly loyal to the Ralston family, even when he didn't necessarily agree with their actions. He'd thought I was a spoiled brat, playing at being a landscaper and not living up to my family's responsibilities, but it hadn't stopped him stepping up to guard me. I'd worked hard to change his opinion of me. I hoped this hadn't changed his mind.

"What would you have me do to two people I count as family? Watch them be made homeless knowing I can make one phone call and let them keep their home?" I saw the conflict in his expression. "Exactly."

Griff huffed. "You take your responsibilities seriously."

"I do." I was a Ralston. What else could I do?

My phone buzzed in my pocket, and I jumped. It was Griff's turn to smirk. I looked at the screen and relaxed when I saw a message from Lily Duchamp asking me to call her.

"Not Mr. Jenner then," Griff drawled.

I glowered at him. "No. How long until we get to the landing strip?"

"Ten minutes."

"I'll call her once we've boarded."

Another buzz. Davy.

"We need to talk." He didn't sound happy.

The screen flashed once more. *"I may want to wring your neck but I'll never be able to thank you enough."*

I let out a breath.

"I'm gonna return every cent."

I smiled at the screen.

"Took it better than you expected?" Griff asked.

"Something like that," I agreed. "He's going to

throttle me and pay the money back."

"Okay." Griff seemed remarkably calm considering someone had just threatened his client.

I messaged Lily to say I'd talk to her shortly, then I messaged Davy to ask if I could talk to him once I got home as Lily wanted to talk now.

He sent a thumbs up emoji and I took a breath in relief. It didn't sound as if the world was going to crash in on my head right now.

It took the three and a half hours of the flight time to thrash out issues with the auction with Lily. I took over the table while Griff sat in one of the big leather chairs. The other two bodyguards retreated to comfortable seats at the back. I was glad I hadn't said I would call Davy too. Lily sounded frazzled and I apologized for leaving her to handle everything while I flew to the farm.

"It's not a problem," Lily assured me. "Greg is here to help me. Now he's not working at the museum, it's freed up his time."

"How's he doing?" I asked cautiously.

"Not good," she admitted, her voice lowering. "The museum was his life. Now he's waiting for everything to fall into place, and he's so fed up."

"Wasn't he starting on his own research?"

I knew Greg had been fired from the museum thanks to the machinations of Lily's mother and he'd not been able to apply for a grant. But now he was going to undertake his own research, selling two of Marisa's paintings to finance the work.

"It's a long story," Lily groaned. "But he's going to start once we've settled near his gran's cottage.

But our cottage needs a remodel. He'll do as much of the work as he can, but first he's helping me. Have you got the green light with the Jenners?"

"I'll know when I get home. One of my handcuffs has offered to help too."

From his chair Griff rolled his eyes.

"Not that big yummy red head?"

I grinned at the muffled protest in the background. Greg did not like his fiancé referring to another man as 'yummy'. I could understand that.

"The very same." I was glad I didn't have the call on speaker. "We can use all the help we can get. The reality is worse than the pictures show."

I heard a tapping noise and wondered if Lily was tapping her nail on the table.

"We could try to get more people if David would let us," she suggested.

"He agreed to Greg, and he's met Griff. Let's not scare him off too much." I could imagine Davy freaking out if a troop of men walked in.

"How did he take you paying the mortgage?"

I hesitated, then said, "About as well as can be expected."

"That good, huh? Did you explain if you hadn't done that there wouldn't have been a place for the animal sanctuary?"

"Can you imagine how that would have gone down?" I said, somewhat defensively.

Lily huffed in my ear. I'd discovered my sweet friend had somewhat of a ruthless streak when it came to this auction. She wanted to get everything, and everyone, organized, and the last thing she wanted was a nasty surprise. She'd spent years watching her mother arrange these events and knew exactly what she was doing. There was a reason I'd asked her for her help. It would have fallen apart left to me.

"We'll get Greg and your handcuff to charm him." Lily suggested.

I looked at Griff doubtfully. Greg may be a 'make love, not war' type. Griff was more of a 'do as you're told' kind of guy.

But then Lily had to finish the conversation, and I had a to-do list as long as my arm just for the auction. When I looked at my emails it tripled in length. I needed to meet with my assistant as soon as we landed. Justin was new to me. He'd recently left Lily's mother's employ. Lily had effected our introduction and said I'd be crazy not to take him on. She was right. He was even more organized than Lily. I was never letting him go.

I called Justin who said he'd be waiting for me when the aircraft landed. I thought about my early morning watching the sun rise over Feather Creek and how my day would end. I added 'call Davy' to the list. I wish I could have ended the day in his arms too. But Elle had to stay on the farm and Elsa had to become a Ralston again.

The private jet bumped as it landed on the airstrip. I wondered idly if I'd ever take a commercial flight again. It was unlikely. This plane was at my private disposal. I'd send it to collect Davy and Robyn when we had the auction. But first, he and I needed to talk. I had my argument formulated. Would it be enough to convince Davy Jenner?

Chapter 13

Davy

The phone call didn't happen that evening. I received a message part way through the evening. It was a picture of someone drowning in paper. I should have been annoyed but it just made me laugh and feel sorry for Elle.

I wasn't surprised when my phone rang as I sat on the stoop in the pre-dawn light, my hands wrapped around a cup of hot chocolate. It was really too cold to be sitting still, but I needed time to think before I started the day's work.

"Morning, Davy."

I frowned at Elle's thin and scratchy voice, nothing like her normal smooth tone. "Are you ill?" I was ready to fly to Boston and bring her some of Momma's chicken noodle soup.

"Just tired," she sighed.

"You sound exhausted. Did you sleep at all?"

She gave a tired laugh. "I haven't been to bed yet. There was a problem which blew up yesterday evening while I was flying back. I didn't get my feet on the ground before we refueled and took off again. We've been fighting fires all night."

"I'm sorry, Elle. Can you sleep now?"

"A couple of hours." She yawned in my ear.

"Sorry." She yawned again and this time I winced as I heard her jaw crack.

"Where are you?" I asked.

"In bed in some hotel. It's not as comfortable as Robyn's bed."

I laughed because she was probably in some five-star luxury hotel and Robyn's bed was as old and tired as could be, but it was really comfortable. "You should sleep. You didn't sleep the previous night either, despite the comfy bed," I teased.

Elle sighed in my ear. Then she yawned again. "Sorry. Sorry."

"You need to sleep, Elle," I said gently.

"I didn't want you to think I was avoiding you."

Maybe I had, for a moment, and now I felt guilty, but she'd made it right. "We can talk when you can think straight."

She hummed in my ear. I wasn't even sure if she was still awake. I sat there listening to the sound of her breathing. She almost startled me when she spoke again.

"What time is it?"

"Sunrise."

Elle sighed. "I wish we were by the creek, Davy. Just you and me."

"I do too." If I had my way, we'd spend every dawn by the creek, watching the sun spread its rays across the land and planning our future together. I'd never let anyone else interfere with our happiness.

"I feel safe in your arms."

She sounded so tired and vulnerable, and I wanted nothing more than to leap on a plane and fly to wherever she was, just so I could hug her. And I'd still take the soup.

"Sleep," I ordered. "I'll stay here and listen until I hear you snoring."

Elle gave a sleepy chuckle. "I don't snore."

"How do you know?" I pointed out.

I didn't know if she snored or not, but Robyn insisted I did.

"I don't," Elle admitted. "I've never slept with anyone. Never kissed anyone except you."

I froze, the cup halfway to my mouth. "There's never been anyone except me?" I queried cautiously.

"I went on dates, but they weren't you, you know? I didn't want to kiss them. You are the only person I wanted to be my husband."

I shut my eyes against the sun peeking over the buildings and once again, cursed under my breath as I thought of time we'd lost because of her grandfather. Elle hadn't been the only girl I'd kissed. But I swiftly realized no one held my attention like she had. I'd resigned myself to spending the rest of my life alone.

I was so lost in my thoughts I initially missed the soft sounds in my ear. Then I grinned. My girl snored.

I listened to her for a long time, not wanting to break the connection between us, until I heard Robyn calling my name. I murmured, "Sleep well, my Elle," and disconnected the call. I tossed the cold remains of the hot chocolate on the dirt floor and went inside to find Robyn.

I didn't have time to do much thinking over the next couple of days. Robyn spent all her time on the office phone, speaking to Elle's assistant, Justin. She didn't have time to tell me what was going on, but I saw the endless lists she made, and she spent all her time with her brows knit together and muttering. Lots of muttering.

I took over her chores on the farm and managed breakfast and supper for us. I had to drag Robyn out of the office to eat which she did with ill-grace. When the last mouthful was finished, she was straight back in the office, only staggering out to fall exhausted into bed, and the whole pattern starting again the following day.

After five days, I put a halt to this when I looked up from my plate at breakfast to discover Robyn had fallen asleep over her cereal. "Okay, lil sis, time you took a nap!"

I hauled Robyn to her feet ignoring her sleepy protests and steered her to her bedroom. She was asleep again before her head hit the pillow. I watched her for a moment to make sure she didn't move, but she didn't even twitch a finger.

I left her bedroom and hunted for my phone which I found on the kitchen dresser. I had a call to make.

"Davy, is everything okay?"

Elle sounded surprised to hear from me. We hadn't spoken since the day I listened to her fall asleep. Robyn had told me Elle and Justin hadn't stopped moving around the country since she returned from the farm. Part of me wondered if that was her family's way of keeping her away from me. I told myself not to be so paranoid, but the concern lingered.

"Davy?" she prompted.

I dragged myself away from my paranoid thoughts and focused on the problem at hand. "Hi Elle. Listen, Robyn needs a break today. Your assistant is wearing her ragged. She's just fallen asleep in her Lucky Charms."

Elle gave a chuckle, but she sounded as weary as Robyn. "He has that effect on everyone. I don't think Justin realizes we don't all work at a hundred miles an hour."

Unseen, I gave a wry smile. That was exactly how Robyn had described him.

"No more phone calls today, I promise," Elle continued. "I'll keep him busy today."

"Thanks, Elle," I said gratefully. "You sound tired yourself."

"I am." She yawned in my ear. "Sorry, I'm making a habit of this. This week has been a nightmare, but it should calm down soon."

"Where are you?"

"I'm..." Elle paused, then she started to laugh. "I've got no idea where I am. The plane has just landed."

"Take some time for yourself, yeah?" I wanted to tell her to come here for a rest, but we didn't have that relationship yet.

"I will, Davy. And don't worry about Robyn. I'll tell Justin to leave her alone today. I think he thought he'd found a soulmate. He said he'd never met anyone as organized as Robyn."

We said goodbye. I thought about what Elle had

just said. I didn't know Justin but I knew he'd worked for one of the most demanding women in Boston. If he thought Robyn was organized that was high praise. Not for the first time, I wondered if I was holding Robyn back keeping her on this little farm.

 I listened at Robyn's door to check she was okay. She was snoring. I grinned and left her to sleep. I had animals to feed.

I made myself a cheese sandwich for lunch and switched on the radio in the kitchen for the news and weather. It was the same radio my grandmother had listened to every day. Somehow it kept going. As I poured myself a tea, I heard a shuffling behind me. I looked over my shoulder to see Robyn sit down at the table, wild-haired, eyes still half-shut, and the outline of her pillow down her cheek. I was tempted to snap a photo and send it to Griff.

"You should have woken me," she grumbled.

"Shut up and drink your coffee." I poured her a cup, and she buried her nose in it.

"I've got so much to do," Robyn said when she came back up for air. She waved vaguely at the cup. I topped off the coffee and sat down at the table.

"Nope," I said firmly. "You're taking a day off. You need to rest."

"But—"

"No buts. I called Elle and told her you were taking a day off. Her assistant can do whatever he needs to by himself."

"But—"

I scowled at her. I don't think Robyn noticed. She still had her eyes closed. "Let's try this again. Go back to bed."

"You need a break too."

I appealed to the only thing I could think of. "Robyn, you won't get to wear the slinky dress made just for you if you've passed out with exhaustion."

"That's blackmail," she muttered.

I grinned. "Is it working?"

"Going."

She stood and shuffled back to her bedroom. I heard the door close and her muffled groan. Robyn had to be exhausted. She never gave in that easily.

I topped off my tea and took it outside with my sandwich to wander over to what was the animal sanctuary. It hurt my heart every time I saw the charred remains, but now, maybe, I had some hope. I knew once the auction was done, we'd get the materials and equipment to start again.

I took a sip of tea and looked up at the clear blue sky. "It's gonna happen, Momma. We'll take care of animals for you. We're gonna get a horse first of all."

I'd almost forgotten about the abused horse, Millie, but Leo had emailed me during the week and asked when he could transport Millie to me. She was coming to us next week. Her stall was ready in the barn. She just needed to get here. Robyn had promised to take care of her, but would she be free, or would Justin still have his claws in her?

I thought about Elle's suggestion of a dude ranch again and shuddered. No, I was more than happy to spend my days giving love to critters who needed our care, but humans were another thing. They could play cowboys on another ranch. I'd looked up dude ranches. Our shabby little farm wouldn't compare to the big ranches where rich city folk stayed.

I took my cup back to the house and left it in the sink. Then I whistled for Bailey and headed to the barn. I wanted to make sure the meadows where Millie would get her freedom were safe from anything that could harm her. I knew they were really. I'd never do anything to put our horses at harm, but Millie relied on us to keep her safe, so I'd do an extra check.

The sound of an engine caught my attention. I frowned as an old Ford pick-up bounced down the road toward me. We didn't get visitors. Aside from Elle. The pick-up stopped and I smiled at our neighbor, Charlie Reedham. I hadn't seen him since the night of the fire.

Chapter 14

Elle

Timing is everything so they say.

Only from the second I left Black Feather farm; my timing was all over the place as I put out fire after fire in various Ralston companies. I didn't sleep beyond catnaps on the plane. I barely had time to eat other than the food Justin thrust at me. I never managed to sit down and have that call with Davy about paying off his mortgage, so when he called me, my heart jumped.

The plane had just landed somewhere. I'd been dozing, desperate to have a few moments rest, when my phone buzzed. The last thing I wanted was to take another call, but it was Davy, who was one of the only people I wanted to talk to—maybe.

When he told me that Robyn was shattered thanks to my wonderful assistant, I groaned inwardly. Justin was amazing. I was never letting this man go. But he never stopped, and he didn't expect anyone else to either. I often wondered why he and Lily's mother had parted company. They were ideally suited.

By the time I finished my call with Davy, we were now in the car en route to somewhere. I looked over at Justin who had a smile playing around his lips.

"Protective older brother?" he asked. He was in his late twenties, a slender, blond-haired man, with a brain that worked a mile a minute. He was usually immaculately dressed, but today he looked as rumpled and tired as I did.

"You're not supposed to wear the recipients into the ground," I teased. "She needs to sleep today, or her older brother will be out for blood."

"But Robyn is so good," he protested.

"As good as you?" I challenged.

To my surprise, Justin nodded. "She could be, with my training. She's wasted where she is."

"Do you usually get the non-profits helping you like this?" I knew he'd worked with Diana Duchamp for years, so it was a genuine question.

Justin shrugged. "There aren't many people who can hold their own with me. Robyn can."

I guess that was a no.

"And I needed her help while we handled this week. It's been a long week." He yawned then.

It was inevitable that I'd give a huge yawn in response. My jaw was sore from the number of times it had cracked. "As soon as we get home for good, you're taking two days to recover."

Justin must have been tired because he didn't protest. "And you?"

I smiled wistfully. "I'd like to go back to Black Feather farm and watch the sunrise over the creek, but I think my mother has events she wants me to attend. I don't think she'd appreciate it if I ran away again."

Justin raised an eyebrow. "Again?"

"Ask me when I'm not so tired." I called it starting a business in a new state, but really it was running away from the man who broke my heart.

He studied me for so long I started to fidget under his intense stare. "You're a fish out of water in Boston, aren't you?"

"What made you guess?" I asked dryly.

He grinned at me. "For a country girl, you're doing okay."

I took it for the compliment it seemed to be. I looked out of the window and blinked as we traveled through the city. "We're home."

"You didn't realize?" Justin's tone was incredulous.

"Davy—David—asked me where we were, and I couldn't tell him," I confessed. "The whole week has been a blur of flights and meetings."

"We both need sleep."

When we reached Ralston House, my mother came out to meet me, dressed in a stunning mauve pantsuit. Since my 'promotion' in the family, Mom always dressed as if she were on the catwalk. She ignored Justin which annoyed me intensely and made a moue as she studied me.

"You need to change, Elsa. You can't go to lunch with the Harcourts dressed like that."

This was the first I'd heard of a lunch date.

I stared at her. "Mom, I haven't slept in a week. The only place I'm going is my bed."

"You can sleep later, darling. It's important that you keep up with our friends."

I sighed, knowing this was going to go one of

two ways and Justin didn't need to watch it. He'd been waiting patiently by the car. I turned to him with a smile. "I'll see you on Monday. I don't need to see you in the office until then."

He inclined his head, picked up his bag, and headed toward the garages where his vehicle was parked.

I turned back to my mother. "Mom, the Harcourts are your friends, not mine."

"And now they can be your friends too," she said brightly.

I took a deep breath, determined to keep my temper. She was my mom and I owed her that. Losing my cool wouldn't help matters, but she had to realize I wasn't at her beck and call now. The Ralston empire had me dancing on their strings. I couldn't be her puppet too. "I know you mean well, but you know the week I've had. I can't remember the last time I slept in a bed and not on the plane. I need to sleep. Please reschedule with the Harcourts or tell them I had a sudden emergency."

"But—"

I leaned forward and kissed her on her powdered cheek. "I love you, Mom. Let me meet your friends when I've rejoined humanity. It will be much better for all of us."

I walked past her before she could protest or coerce me. Inside the house, my father smiled and came over to hug me. "Well handled, Elle. Go to bed before your mom realizes what you've done."

He kissed me on the cheek and nudged me toward the stairs. I climbed them wearily and flopped facedown onto my bed. It was huge and comfortable, and not the bed I wanted to sleep in.

I pulled my phone out of my pocket and stabbed at the screen with one eye half open.

"Elle."

His deep rumbling voice was exactly what I needed to hear. So much so that my eyes stung with sudden emotion.

"Hi Davy. I wanted to let you know I know where I am now."

Startled silence. It went on for so long I squinted at the phone to see if the connection had dropped. Then he guffawed. I grinned. It wasn't often Davy let go like that.

"Where are you?" he asked when he'd stopped laughing.

"In my bed. I hadn't noticed we landed in Boston," I admitted sheepishly.

Davy barked out another laugh, then he said, and his voice was amused but tender, "You need to sleep."

"I do," I admitted, "but I just wanted to hear your voice."

"I'm glad you called. It feels like a lifetime since you left."

I sucked in a breath. I would never have to hide my feelings from Davy. He just came right out and said what he thought. I owed him that same frank honesty. "I wish I was with you."

"I wish you were here too," he said in a low rumble. "When are you coming back?"

"I don't know," I sighed.

"Millie arrives on Wednesday. Do you want to

meet your girl?"

I rolled over onto my back and smiled up at the ceiling. "If I can squeeze in a day without a crisis I'll be there. It'll be good to see Leo again too."

I blinked. Did Davy just grunt? "You know Leo liked Robyn, right? He wasn't interested in me."

Davy huffed in my ear. "I'm being ridiculous, aren't I?"

"Yes, but I like the fact you're jealous."

I expected him to splutter, to deny he was jealous, but he didn't. I should have remembered Davy didn't play those kinds of games.

"I'm only jealous when I think of you," he admitted.

"I only see you."

He sucked in his breath. "You don't want the men in their sharp suits."

I furrowed my brow in confusion and then I realized he meant the men at the charity auction. "Lily calls them sharks, all large mouths and sharp teeth."

He laughed. "That's a good name for them."

"Her mother keeps trying to marry her off to a shark, even though she's with Greg. I hope my mother doesn't get that idea."

"You can tell her the sharks would be wasting their time."

Was that a smug smirk I could sense? I wish I could see him.

I settled further into the pillows. Sleep was dragging me down. One day I'd like to have a conversation with him when I wasn't falling asleep.

As if he sensed how tired I was, he said, "Sleep now, sweetheart."

I gasped. Did he just call me his sweetheart?

"Too much?" he asked.

"Not too much," I assured him.

Just as I thought we were going to say goodbye, Davy said, "Do you know Charlie Reedham?"

I furrowed my brow. "Why do I know that name?"

"Reedham's have the property bordering ours. Wildcat Ranch."

It took me a moment. I was so tired. Then I snapped my fingers. "Didn't Jo Beth Reedham go to grade school with us?"

"She did," Davy agreed. "Charlie's her older brother from her father's first marriage."

"I remember him. I didn't like him. He was always leering at the girls." Charlie was one of the reasons I spent so much time with the Jenners. He would never leave me alone. But I wasn't about to tell Davy that. "Why are you talking about him?"

"Charlie paid me a visit earlier in the week. He's not very happy that you paid off the mortgage. He'd been waiting for the bank to foreclose so he could snap the farm up at auction."

I sat up, running my fingers through his hair. "What did he say?"

Davy hesitated.

"Did he threaten you?" I demanded.

"It's nothing I can't handle, Elle. He's all mouth, is all."

I knew Davy well enough to know he was

deflecting. I'd make a few phone calls to find out the information I needed.

"Be careful, Davy," I insisted. "Make sure you call Sheriff Hernández if Charlie starts threatening you."

"I'll be fine, Elle."

I wanted to tell him I could handle it. The sheriff had a fine new office thanks to my family. But that would be like throwing gasoline on the flames. So instead I kept quiet and let him wish me a long and uninterrupted sleep. I murmured and sounded sleepier than I really was now. I would sleep, but first I had calls to make.

Chapter 15

Davy

I cursed my impulse for sharing Charlie Reedham's visit with Elle. She needed sleep, but I knew that she'd be on the phone with Sheriff Hernández second we disconnected the call. The sheriff was in Ralston's pocket, as was every other institution in the area. Elle didn't have to tell me that. But Reedham had clout in these parts. I doubted Hernández would roll over for Elle.

I was more worried about Charlie Reedham's visit than I was going to admit to Elle. Especially now I knew we stood in the way of his plans. He was a shrewd and ambitious man, more successful at running his ranch than I'd ever been. He needed more land, and Black Feather farm would have been a perfect addition to his ranch. He'd waited patiently for us to fail. Even helped us when we had the fire. He came to Momma's funeral and mourned with us. All the while knowing it was the nail in our coffin.

But when he found out Elle had saved us, that's when he lost it. He'd offered to buy the farm for a fraction of its value. When I refused his offer Reedham had screamed and shouted in my face. I'd tried to keep my cool, but it had been hard.

Then he'd stood back and told me to take care of my pretty little sister. That had scared me more than anything else. He could threaten me. I didn't care. He couldn't hurt Elle, or her handcuffs would tear him apart. But he could hurt Robyn.

By the time morning arrived, I didn't know what to do, so I walked out to the paddock and called the one man who could help me.

Griff listened as I stumbled through Reedham's visit. "Already on it, Davy. We're checking him out now."

Why was I not surprised? Elle would have called him first. "You are?"

"I think he's all hot air and bluster, but I'm not risking you or Robyn. He will be getting a visit."

Griff didn't say who by and I didn't ask.

"He could cause us trouble," I admitted. "He didn't want us to build the animal sanctuary, and now I know why."

"Leave it with me, Davy. Just keep a watch for anything unusual."

"I will."

I'd just disconnected the call when the screen lit up. Greg, Lily's boyfriend.

"Hello?"

"Davy, how are you?" Greg said, his greeting cheerful as ever.

They all called me Davy now. Once upon a time I'd have insisted he called me David. Davy was a kid's name. But since Elle came back into my life I didn't care.

"Hey, Greg. Aren't you supposed to be working?"

It was an old joke now. Greg still hadn't started his research.

"Soon. The remodel is almost finished. My sister wants to fly down to fit Robyn's dress, or something like that. Do you want me to come with her and clear the area for the rebuild?"

"You're bored, aren't you?"

"Out of my head," he confessed. "Lily keeps finding me work to do for the auction. I thought I was gifting a painting, not being one of the hired help. She's just like her mother."

I grinned. "Have you told her that?"

"I'm not that stupid. Do you want me there or not?"

"Yeah, come down. I gotta warn you, one of my neighbors is causing trouble."

I thought it was only fair to give him the heads up.

"Then you need an extra body there," Greg said cheerfully.

I huffed out a breath. I should have said no, but I appreciated the extra pair of hands. Greg was never afraid to get stuck into the work.

"I do. Thanks, Greg. Uh, you know this place. Designer dresses are gonna get covered in dirt."

"It's cool. My sister has it all worked out with Robyn. They're both frighteningly organized."

I knew nothing about his sister other than she designed amazing dresses. But when Robyn mentioned she was wearing a Valerie Crenshaw dress to folks here, I'd heard some *oohs* and *aahs* and *"You lucky thing!"* It was the first time I'd ever seen Robyn preen.

"When are you getting here?" I asked.

"Tomorrow. We can only stay two days because Valerie has to get home for a show."

"That works. We've got a horse arriving on Wednesday."

"Millie?" Greg laughed. "Good luck with that one."

"You've met Millie?"

"Once. I love horses but Millie is too much, even for me."

That didn't inspire me with confidence.

"See you tomorrow."

I disconnected the call and looked at my phone.

"Lunch."

"Soup."

"Chocolate cake."

"Where are you?"

"Davy, Davy, Davy!"

"Have you been kidnapped by aliens?"

I laughed. I could answer that one. *"Yes."*

"Ok."

"I'll have your cake."

No way. That cake was mine. *"Touch my cake and you're in trouble."*

The phone buzzed.

"Too late," Robyn sing-songed. "I've eaten it all."

I disconnected the call and stomped over to the house. I found a bowl of homemade soup and bread, and a large piece of chocolate cake, on the table.

"I knew you were lying," I yelled.

"You were lucky," I yelled back. "Oh no, Justin, I didn't mean you. Unless you're lucky too."

I grinned as I sat down. I couldn't wait to tell Elle all about that conversation.

I was checking one of the ewes who'd seemed off-color the day before when Greg and Valerie arrived. The ewe was from one of our rare breeds and I was concerned I would have to call out the vet. But she seemed fine now. I'd keep an eye on her though. I couldn't afford to let her go downhill. I took the time to check all the other sheep in case it was a poison or a virus. But I couldn't see any sign of infection. They all looked fine. I breathed a sigh of relief. I didn't want to be faced with a veterinary bill yet.

I checked the chickens too. They were as loud and annoying as ever, but none of them seemed ill. I chatted to them all and collected one or two eggs I'd missed that morning.

"Do you always talk to the chickens?" Greg asked, sounding amused.

I looked up from an in-depth conversation with my favorite chicken, Della. "Don't you talk to your plants?" I challenged.

"I do," Greg admitted. "All the time. I don't usually discuss sheep's illnesses with them."

"What do you talk about?"

"How much I love Lily," Greg confessed.

That was sweet. Sappy, but sweet. It wasn't like I hadn't discussed Elle with all my animals.

"It's good to see you, Greg." I held out the eggs to show him why I couldn't shake hands.

"And you," Greg said. "We've been told to stay out of the house for a couple of hours while Valerie fits the dress. You've got me here. Why don't I get started?"

"Sounds good to me. I'll join you once I've finished here."

"Still got to finish your conversation?" Greg asked, not bothering to hide his huge grin.

"Something like that," I said. "Go away while I tell Della what a pretty girl she is."

Greg smirked as he waved, then vanished toward the new barn.

"He doesn't understand," I told Della.

She bawked at me. Della understood just fine.

Greg and I worked until dusk clearing away the site of the animal sanctuary. I'd been unable to touch it for a long time, the pain in my heart too much just looking at it. But now there was hope and a rebirth. I let Greg take the lead and between us we got it ready for rebuilding.

"How did the fire start?" Greg asked as he stretched and rolled his shoulders.

"A rodent nibbled at a cable," I said. "Started an electrical fire."

He hummed and I turned to look at him.

"What's the hum for?"

"Did you find the cable?"

"We found the remains of the rodent by the cable," I said. I couldn't read Greg's expression. "Tell me what you're thinking."

"I think your fire was started deliberately."

I walked over to where he pointed. It was a length of cable with teeth marks.

"Yeah, that looks about right." I couldn't remember what had happened to the cable.

"Look at the cable, Davy. It wasn't attached to anything. It didn't burn because it was buried by something."

I stared at him, unease coiling in my gut. "You mean..." I didn't want to say the words out loud.

Greg gave a grim nod. "Whoever started this wanted you to think it was an accident."

We cleared up and walked back to the house. I stowed the cable in the new barn and asked Greg not to say anything to anyone, especially Lily. If he told her, she would tell Elle. I needed time to process this.

Greg didn't look happy, but he nodded. "Okay, but don't leave it too long. You need to talk to Sheriff Hernández about this."

"I will, but I think I might know who did this, but I don't have any proof, yet."

I would get the proof. I just had no idea how. And then we'd have to deal with the fallout.

Robyn looked so happy when I walked in, there was no way I was going to destroy her happiness with something that might not be true. I would talk to Griff later and let him investigate.

"Can I see the dress?" I asked.

"Not until the day," Valerie said. "And you boys need to wash up."

I didn't need to be introduced. She looked just like her brother, only dressed elegantly and a lot cleaner.

"We'd better do it. She'll only complain," Greg said, in a loud whisper. "You know what big sisters are like."

"I have a little sister. Does that count?" I asked.

There may have been more than a decade between them, but Robyn and Valerie perfected the art of the scathing eye roll.

Over dinner, Valerie told us scandalous, heavily redacted, stories about her clients. Robyn and I had no clue who they might have been about, but they were very funny. Greg told us about weekends with his grandparents in Maine. And we talked about living here all our lives; the good, the bad, and the ugly.

If it hadn't been for the find of the piece of cable, it would have been one of the most fun and most relaxing evenings I'd had in a long time.

Chapter 16

Elle

Despite the companies' best efforts to thwart me, I arrived just ahead of Millie. I'd hoped to see her before the road trip, but it wasn't to be. However, the SUV arrived in the yard about thirty minutes before Leo's old horsebox.

I'd had a tussle with Justin to schedule in Millie time. Justin didn't understand how important Millie was to me. His eyeroll and "She's just a horse," did not go down well, but after an intense discussion and his apology, we came out with a better understanding.

Robyn had assured me I didn't need to be there, but I couldn't let my girl be moved without her knowing I cared enough to ensure she was all right. I'd rescued Millie. It was my job to make certain she would be happy at Black Feather farm. I wasn't sure what we'd do if she didn't settle. Leo couldn't take her back. That was a worry for another day.

As I got out of the vehicle, I smiled at Davy and Robyn who met us in the yard. "Are you as nervous as I am?"

"A little," Robyn agreed. "This is our first sanctuary resident."

Davy smiled at me. "Millie will be fine here, Elle. She's come to the right place to live out her days."

I wish I were as calm as him. I remembered her first reaction to Leo's fine stables. There were moments we all thought the worst.

We sat on the stoop while the handcuffs did their usual check around the farm. Davy was used to it by now, so he didn't scowl as he had done in my early visits.

They returned but instead of disappearing into the bunkhouse, they headed down the drive.

Davy turned to me. "What are they doing?"

"They'll check the horsebox before it gets here. I told Leo so he knows what to expect."

"You take it so calmly," he muttered.

"It's my life," I said, patting his knee. "It's not like anything is going to happen to me. I had to tell them about Charlie Reedham, but Griff has gotten that covered. It's just to tick the boxes."

"If it means I get to see Griff, I don't mind," Robyn said. She flushed as we both rolled our eyes. "You're both mean to me."

She sounded so like the preteen I remembered; I couldn't help but giggle. She flushed deeper and almost shoved me off the steps. Davy laughed at both of us.

Finally, we heard the loud rumbling sound of Leo's old horsebox. I'd offered to buy him a new one as thanks for boarding Millie. He'd turned me down flat. Men and their pride.

Davy got to his feet and brushed off his butt. He looked down at both of us. "Let's go meet your girl."

I sucked in a calming breath. I really hoped my girl was on her best behavior. Millie could be a pain if she was in the right mood.

Davy hauled me to my feet. "She'll be fine, Elle. You'll see."

Leo came to a halt, and jumped out, a huge smile on his face. The gangly teenager had grown into a tall, handsome, sandy-haired man with a ready smile. He hugged me, then turned to Davy. "Davy Jenner, it's good to see you again and it's so good to be back at Black Feather farm. I wish I could have brought my wife." He shook Davy's hand and clapped his back. Then he turned to Robyn. "Robyn, so good to see you too. Have you forgiven me for the bluebonnets?"

She laughed and reached up to kiss his cheek. "Just don't do it again."

"I promise. My wife would kill me if I gave another woman flowers."

"As she should," Robyn agreed. "Your wife is welcome here any time. Can we meet Millie?"

Leo grimaced. "She's in a bit of a mood."

"We'll take it slow," Davy assured him. "Her stall is ready, away from the others."

We all stayed clear as Leo unloaded the palomino paint horse. Millie wasn't going to come easily. Eventually she agreed to walk calmly down the ramp. I wanted to rush over and say hello to my pretty girl, but I knew better than to do that. Her body language screamed how unsettled she was.

"She's so lovely," Robyn cooed. "What a lovely

girl."

We let Leo fuss over her and remove her travel boots when she was calm enough, then he led her to her stall.

Leo smiled in relief when he rejoined us. "That went a lot easier than I expected."

I nodded in agreement. "If you remember what she was like when she came to you."

He grimaced. "I thought it was going to fail from the start."

I looked over to Davy and Robyn, and caught the odd expression on Davy's face. Almost as if he were jealous at us talking about past times. I smiled at him, and he relaxed enough to return it. One day I would convince him that there had only ever been one man for me.

"Come in the house, Leo. Lunch is ready," Robyn said. "You can meet my boyfriend."

"He's not that huge man mountain by the gate, is he?" Leo had been joking but when Robyn nodded, he shivered. "Tell him I'm a make love, not war, kind of guy."

"I think he'll get that," Robyn assured him.

Leo gave her a hard stare, then grinned. "I guess I deserved that."

"Just a little," she agreed.

They walked across the yard, still ribbing each other.

"Sometimes I forget my sister is all growed up," Davy murmured.

"Don't worry. She'll keep reminding you," I said.

The introduction between Griff and Leo eased

considerably when Griff realized Leo was happily married, and didn't hesitate to talk about his wife and laugh at himself.

We were drinking sun tea when Robyn said, "Why is she called Millie?"

"She didn't have a name," I said. "It was the first one I thought of."

"Could we change it to fit in with the others?"

"What were you thinking?" Davy asked.

"Peardrop."

Davy raised an eyebrow. "Why Peardrop?"

"Because of the shape of the blaze on her nose. Look."

Robyn got her cell phone out and passed it around. When it reached me, I studied the photo of Millie. The white blaze did look like a pear drop.

"I don't see why not," I said and was rewarded with a beaming smile from Robyn.

Davy shrugged. "She's part of the family so why not."

Leo left soon after lunch and I went to see the newly named Peardrop.

Peardrop fussed a little when she saw me, but after a while she responded to my voice and came over to greet me.

"You're going to be so happy here," I told her. "This is the best place in the world."

She tossed her head, but maybe she listened too because she stayed calm.

I turned to see Davy grinning at me. "The best place in the world, huh?"

I raised an eyebrow. "You disagree?"

"No, I think you're about right. This is the best place in the world...now you're here."

I wished I could stay forever.

By the time I'd dressed and reached the kitchen the next morning, Davy had disappeared, but the coffeepot was almost full. I poured a cup and headed outside. As he wasn't on the stoop, I knew where he'd be. Sure enough, I found him lurking by what had been the animal sanctuary, but he was talking to Griff. Bailey was at their feet.

Davy and Greg had cleared the area and it was ready to be rebuilt. As soon as the auction was held, the building materials would be purchased. It wouldn't take long to reconstruct.

Griff waved when he saw me. "Morning, Elsa. I'm going for a walk. Come on, Bailey."

To my surprise, Bailey trotted after him.

Davy took a swallow of coffee as I joined him. "Hey, did I wake you up?"

I shook my head. "That would have been the call at four thirty. I'd just finished when I heard you get up. Sorry, I didn't mean to disturb your conversation with Griff."

"We were done. Do they ever let you sleep through the night?"

His expression was so fierce and protective, it made me smile. "Not often. It's my own fault. I told them I wanted to be kept involved in everything. I think I can let go of the reins though. My grandfather employed good people. They know what they're doing. What are you doing out here?"

"I couldn't sleep, and I needed time to think. I've been to see Peardrop. She's moody in the morning. Just like you."

I growled at him, and he chuckled.

"Are you worrying about the auction?" I wrapped my hands around my own coffee. It was chilly this morning, and our breaths were clearly visible in the morning air. I shivered.

"You should have worn a jacket," he chided, putting his arm around my shoulders, and drawing me against him for extra warmth.

I huddled in gratefully. "I didn't think about the cold. So what are you thinking about so hard, it's keeping you awake at night?"

Davy huffed and stared up at the sky. "Why would people want to help a small farm in Texas?"

"They don't," I said, regretting my blunt words as he flinched. "It's the animal sanctuary that's the draw. You know what people are like about animals in need."

He grunted and drained his cup. Then he said, "Thanks for believing in me—in us."

"I never stopped, Davy."

We stood in silence for a long time, until I'd finished my coffee and it was really too cold to stand there any longer. Then we went inside to find Robyn and Griff sat at the kitchen table.

I eyed the toast and Robyn sighed.

"Help yourself. I'll make more."

"They could make their own," Griff grumbled.

Davy and I ignored him, helping ourselves to the toast and smearing it with Robyn's homemade butter. I discovered that Davy made the bread when I complimented Robyn.

"Davy's much better at making bread than I am," Robyn said. "You could use my loaves as doorstops."

"That's true," Davy agreed. "But I can't make pastry."

As Robyn launched into a tale of Davy's disastrous pastry, I wondered if Davy and Robyn made everything because they hadn't been able to afford to buy groceries or because they liked cooking. I looked up and saw the pity in Griff's eyes. He seemed to be thinking the same thing. I couldn't remember Momma Jenner making her own bread and butter.

"Hey." Davy leaned forward and placed his large hand over mine. "I can see what you're thinking. It's okay. Robyn and I have been making our own bread and butter for years."

Robyn nodded. "We discovered we were good at it, and it saved us money."

"It tastes better than what I buy," Griff agreed, helping himself to more toast. He eyed them both speculatively.

"Next time we'll give you supplies to take home," she assured him.

"Next time we'll give him the recipe," Davy said, and chuckled at Griff's grimace.

"Justin wants to know if we're ready for the auction," Robyn said. "I told him I was, but Davy was cowering in a corner."

Davy gave a rueful smile. "If that wasn't true, I'd be offended."

"You'll be fine," I told him. "How's your speech

coming along."

He dropped the knife he'd just picked up and stared at me, open-mouthed. "Speech? What speech?"

Chapter 17

Davy

"If you run away now, I'll set the handcuffs on you," Elle murmured, her hand on my lower back, her copper dress a rustle of silk behind me.

How did she know my first instinct was to run?

"I know you, Davy Jenner."

Now she just sounded amused. Did I say that out loud?

"There are so many people here." I said, uncomfortably aware just how close to a whiny child I sounded.

"And they're all here to see you," she said cheerfully.

Now I really wanted to escape.

She stopped and pulled me to one side, ignoring the murmurs behind us. "May I give you some advice?" Now she was all Elsa.

I gave a curt nod.

"Everyone is going to want to talk to you about the thing that matters most to you, and that's the sanctuary. So channel Momma Jenner and think about what she wanted. Tell them about your momma, about why she wanted the sanctuary in the first place. By the time you've told that story half a dozen times, you'll wonder why you were nervous in the first place."

"Momma. Sanctuary. I can do this."

"I can't do this," Robyn said behind us, her voice quavering.

I looked at my beautiful sister, her titian hair tumbling over one shoulder, and dressed in a deep blue, the color of the skies back home. Valerie had done her proud.

"You look so beautiful," I told her. "Daddy would be so proud."

Her nervousness was pushed away for a moment as she smiled at me. "So do you."

Elle had kept her promise to me and ignored all suggestions of a tuxedo. I wore the whitest shirt I'd ever seen, dress pants that almost looked like jeans and a smart jacket. I'd allowed a stylist to trim my hair and give me a wet shave.

"No one would recognize me back home," I joked.

When Elle put a Stetson on my head, I objected. "This is nothing like my hat."

She just smiled at me and told me I'd be grateful later.

Robyn clutched my arm. "There are so many people."

I loosened her grip and tucked her hand in the crook of my elbow, saying, "We go out there and tell them about our momma and why she wanted to build the sanctuary."

"We do?" Robyn sounded uncertain.

I nodded. "Our momma was a good woman. They'll understand that once we've told them."

Robyn took a deep breath. "You're right. We

can do this—for Momma."

"Got your boots on?" Elle asked, raising her dress to show off her copper boot.

We grinned at each other and stuck out one leg to compare boots. They may not have been our work boots, but they were comfortable.

"We can do this." I took a deep breath and faced the door. Elle put her hand on my back again and I made an effort to relax. This was for Momma.

It was nerve-racking, but by the time I'd told the story to the third or fourth power couple, I felt better. Channeling my momma was a great idea. Elle was right. Unlike last time, these people were here to see us, and I owed it to them and their wallets to give them a story. They all cooed over the Stetson, and I saw the smirk on Elle's face more than once when someone mentioned it.

Not everyone was happy to be here. One of the things my momma always said I was good at was recognizing a sick animal. I could spot the way an animal moved, the way it reacted to other people. I could handle Peardrop because I recognized in her, the same kind of need. She had been wounded deeply by others and just needed careful handling.

I didn't always have the same gift with humans, but in this case, the man stood out like a sore thumb. He was a waiter and he carried out his duties efficiently enough, but there was something about him that alerted my attention.

I watched him for a while. He was maybe in his

thirties, about five feet ten, and developing a gut. I'm not sure whether it was his pinched face or the tremor of his hands I noticed first. I wasn't going to label a guy just for having shaking hands. Maybe he did like a drop too much, but he didn't smell of liquor and he managed the plates. He was very attentive of Elle and her family, but then they all were. No one wanted to upset the Ralstons.

So what was bothering me? I wasn't sure until I looked deep into his eyes. The man had the same wounded expression that Peardrop did. Someone had hurt this man dearly. And just like Peardrop, he was dangerous. I didn't know how I knew. I just did.

"What's worrying you?" Griff asked. The man could walk so quietly. He'd come up behind my chair and I hadn't even noticed. "You're very preoccupied."

"The waiter," I murmured. "The one with graying hair at the temples."

"I see him. What's bothering you?"

"I don't know," I confessed, "but there's something not right about him."

I expected Griff to laugh, but he didn't.

"We'll investigate," Griff said.

I saw him check the guy out without being obvious about it. Then he was gone.

"What's wrong?" Elle asked, leaning closer to me, and I inhaled her light perfume.

"Nothing," I lied. "Griff was just checking I wasn't about to escape."

Her chuckle made me smile. "We'd better get

started with the speeches and the auction."

I groaned. "Do we have to?"

"That's what you're here for, cowboy." Elle tipped my Stetson.

"You made me wear this just so you could annoy me, didn't you?" I said sourly.

Elle's smile was positively wicked.

I'd thought Elle was joking when she said I had to give a speech. I'd suggested Robyn in my place, who'd looked at me in horror and told me they were crazy thoughts. I thought she'd be much better than me, but I didn't get a choice.

Elle had given me the basics. Thank everyone for being there. Tell them how grateful Robyn and I were. Thank Elle and Lily for all their hard work. Thank the Ralston family. *Yeah, that one stuck in my craw.* Encourage them to spend a lot. Laugh.

She added one more as I stood on trembling legs to take my place at the podium. "Tell them about your momma."

I was sensing a theme here. I walked to the podium and stared out at the sea of people. I tried to imagine them naked. That didn't work. So I imagined them as my sheep and chickens, and that worked better. I took a deep breath.

"My name is David Jenner. I own a small farm in Texas and a year ago my momma asked me to build an animal sanctuary. Some of you will have heard about her already this evening." I heard a ripple of laughter. I turned to Elle and winked at her. She smiled. My grin faded when I noticed the waiter's eyes fixed on Elle. After my speech I was going to find out what was his problem. I took a deep breath and turned back to the audience.

It wasn't the best speech, but I saw more than one woman dab her eyes as I told them about Momma dying of a broken heart when the sanctuary burned down. When I told them how Elle and Lily had come together for us, the applause resounded in the room. Elle and Lily stood and waved, and I walked over to brush my lips over the back of their hands.

"You're wooing them tonight." Lily's grin was huge.

I raised an eyebrow. "Isn't that what I'm supposed to do?"

"I thought you'd be all nervous."

"I'm terrified," I confessed. "I'm imagining them as my critters."

Her laughter peeled out. "I'm going to do that when it's my turn. But we'll get you back again. You're a star."

"Never," I said fervently. There was no chance I would ever do this again.

"Finish your speech," Elle urged, "and we'll get on with the auction."

"Come with me?" I asked and held out my hand.

She smiled, threaded her fingers through mine, and we walked back to the podium. I finished my speech, telling them about Peardrop, aware of all eyes on our joined hands. I even make a joke about our boots. Then I went back to my seat, trying not to rush, while Elle introduced Lily, who was going to hold the auction.

I had no idea how much money we were going

to raise. I remembered the auctions I'd been to as a kid. They weren't about luxury items. I watched as people's homes and possessions were sold, leaving them with nothing. The air of defeat was overwhelming.

This was nothing like that. These people were prepared to *spend*. I now understood why Lily argued so fiercely for the amount of champagne on the tables.

Robyn's eyes grew wider and wider as the bids went up on one of the smaller items. "What on earth?" she hissed to me. "Momma would be horrified. They could buy this for a buck 99 in Walmart."

I tried hard not to burst into howling laughter. She was right, but I doubt they'd find any of these items in Walmart.

We sat back and watched the auction proceed, although most of my attention was on Griff who was obviously worried about something.

I don't know how much the auction raised, but I know Marisa Rosen's 'Lost' painting went for over seven figures. No one seem shocked except for Robyn and me.

As soon as the auction was finished Lily and Elle were claimed by people wanting to talk to them.

"I'm going to find the bathroom," I said, patting Robyn's shoulder.

I went to use the facilities, then edged my way into the ballroom, stopping when people wanted to talk to me and wish me luck with the new sanctuary. I couldn't help the slight edge of bitterness as I remembered the way we were ignored the last time. But then I told myself to get over it. That was then. This was now.

I reached Robyn who was deep in conversation with an older man who looked familiar.

"This is Greg's father," Robyn said as I reached them.

"Mr. Crenshaw." I held out my hand.

Greg's father smiled as we shook hands. "Good to meet you, Mr. Jenner. Greg's done nothing but talk about your animal sanctuary."

"Call me Davy," I said. "You're welcome to come with him any time."

"I will. With pleasure." He seemed genuinely pleased at the invitation. "I need to find my wife."

"She's over there," Robyn said, and Greg's father headed after her.

As I turned to look for Elle, I spotted the waiter rushing toward her, and I knew without a doubt, he intended to hurt her.

"Robyn, get away from here and find Griff. Tell him it's happening. Now!"

To my surprise she took one look at my expression and did as I asked, heading toward the door to be met by one of Griff's team. They all knew who she was. No one would let Robyn be hurt.

Once I knew she was safe, I focused all my attention on the waiter. Elle hadn't noticed him. As he aimed the gun at Elle, I moved, and before he could fire, I stood in front of her, blocking his aim.

It took him a moment to realize what I'd done.

"Get out of my way. I don't have a problem with you." He waved the gun, but I stayed where I was.

"What are you doing?" she hissed, her hand on my back. "Davy, it's me he wants. Not you."

I stayed exactly where I was, not taking my eyes off the man for a second. "I'm not letting anyone threaten you, Elle. I love you."

Chapter 18

Elle

"Get out of the way," the man screamed.

"I can't do that, friend." Davy's voice was as calm as could be. Like facing a madman with a gun was an everyday occurrence.

I wanted to throw up. The man pointed a gun at the love of my life and Davy wouldn't get out of the way. I could see black-clad men guiding people out of the room. The guests were so calm. These were the top echelon used to security. They'd been trained for this. Davy, on the other hand, was a rural farmer. No one pointed a gun at him.

I saw Robyn protesting, wanting to stay with Davy, but Griff was firm and she went under protest. I hoped that wouldn't come back to bite him on the butt.

"I'm not your friend," the man snapped. "Get out of the way and let me take the girl. No one needs to get hurt."

"You put down the gun," Davy ordered. "They don't care about me, but they're not gonna let you get out of here with Ms. Ralston."

It was a fair assessment. Security had cleared the room in a remarkably short time and my handcuffs had weapons trained on the gunman. Did he even notice? He wouldn't get out of the room alive unless he put the gun down. I processed this even as Davy and the man talked. It kept me from falling apart. How had this happened? How had the man gotten in the house? I knew Griff would be furious.

What if the man shot Davy?

"Davy, please—" I started but the man screamed at me to shut up.

He wasn't stable, that was obvious. Sweat beaded his forehead and his hands shook. I was worried about the gun going off accidentally. He kept looking at the door. At first I thought he was waiting for his team, but I realized he was waiting for the police. The handcuffs didn't seem to register with him at all. The only thing I was sure of was the man wasn't a professional. Davy would be dead by now and I'd have been abducted, the possibility of survival remote. I knew the stats. Griff had drilled it into my head over and over. Ironic that I was now in danger by an amateur.

"What's your name?" Davy asked.

"Why?" the man snarled.

"So we can talk. My name's Davy Jenner."

"Chris Whitely."

Definitely an amateur if he gave up his name so easily.

"Why do you want to do this, Chris?" Davy asked.

"They killed my wife and left my kids without their momma."

I blinked. "Your wife?" I asked as gently as I

could. I didn't want to trigger Whitely.

"You know what you did," he snarled.

"I don't know," I said. "I'm so sorry. I'm new. But tell me what happened."

The gun wavered again. "You're lying."

"She's not," Davy said. "When did your wife die, Chris?"

"She died six months ago. Cancer. In a hospital owned by her. Because she didn't give my wife the right treatment." Whitely pointed a finger at me.

"Elle was a gardener until old man Ralston died. She wasn't the one responsible for your wife's death."

That seemed to shake Whitely, but he shook his head. "It doesn't matter. Her family's still responsible."

"But killing Elle won't help," Davy said gently. "You shoot her, and your kids will be left with no momma or daddy."

"They have their aunt. She's gotten custody now."

I understood he never expected to come back alive. He was a desperate man with nothing left to lose. "Mr. Whitely. Would you let me investigate what happened to your wife?"

Whitely's lip curled. "Why would you do that?"

"Because a good friend of mine lost his momma and I couldn't help him."

Davy jolted as he realized I meant him.

Whitely hesitated, his attention wavering, and his gun lowered. The handcuffs were on him in a split-second, forcing him to the ground. He didn't resist and I saw the defeated expression in his eyes, an expression I'd seen in Davy's eyes at the first gala.

"I promise you I'll check," I told him as he was handcuffed and led away.

Whitely didn't react, didn't look at me. He was broken.

Before Whitely was led out of the room, Davy had turned to face me and I'd collapsed into his arms, shaking like a leaf. He held me close against him, stroking my hair and murmuring in my ear until I'd gotten myself under control. I don't even know what he said, but the soft words comforted me and finally I stopped shaking. He didn't let go of me though, and I was glad of his muscular arms around me.

I don't know how long we stood like that until I heard a cough behind me. I dabbed at my eyes, hoping I hadn't smeared my eye make-up, and turned to see Griff's grim face. Then I noticed his grimness was aimed at Davy, not me.

"What do you think you were doing?" he barked. "You told me about Whitely."

I turned to Davy. "You knew there was something wrong?"

They both ignored me.

Griff leaned into Davy who looked genuinely confused. "You could have gotten yourself killed."

"Whitely was going to shoot Elle," Davy said as though it were obvious.

"So you thought you'd take the bullet instead?"

Davy shrugged. "He wasn't going to hurt my girl."

My heart skipped a beat at his casual 'my girl'.

Griff was not swayed by this argument. "It's my job to take the bullet, you idiot. We could have neutralized the situation and removed Elsa from the room. Instead you got in the way."

Davy's face hardened. "Neutralized. You mean killed him."

"If necessary."

I knew Griff would never apologize for his job, nor would I expect him to. I laid a hand on Davy's forearm, asking without words for him to stay calm. I felt the muscles clench under my touch.

"Davy did what he thought was right, and Griff, you have a job to do. Neither of you are wrong. You just have different priorities." I knew I was right when they both scowled at me. "Griff, he needed help, not a bullet. What I want to know is how he got in here."

"I can answer that," Griff huffed. "He took a job as a waiter with the catering company."

I furrowed my brow. "How did he know about the auction?"

"He's worked for them for months. Needs the money, I guess. This event came up and he saw his chance to attack the family he blamed for his wife's death."

I sighed and Davy gathered me into his arms.

"What a mess," I said. "We need to make sure his children are taken care of. There's an aunt?"

"On it," Griff said. He left with a final scowl at Davy who huffed.

I looked up at him. "Thank you for saving me, Davy Jenner."

"At least someone appreciates me," he

grumbled.

"I appreciate you," I assured him. "Your sister, not so much." I laughed at Davy's groan as Robyn stalked across the ballroom toward him. "You're in trouble."

"David Leslie Jenner," Robyn bellowed. "What did you think you were doing?"

"Hide me," he begged.

Justin grinned at us when I guided Davy and Robyn into my office the next morning. "Fun night?"

"Heh." He knew as well as I did exactly what sort of night we'd had seeing as he'd been there.

"Are we going to have to hold the auction again?" Robyn asked. Her face was almost white under her bright hair, and she looked as exhausted as I felt.

Justin knit his brows. "Why would we have to do that?"

It was her turn to look confused. "Because of what happened."

Justin chuckled and drew her over to look at his tablet. "I think you'll be fine."

Her jaw dropped. "Are you serious?"

I knew what she was looking at, so I didn't move. "Show Davy."

"I don't think we'll have to worry about financing the sanctuary for a while," Robyn said, her voice strangled. She took the tablet over to Davy and pointed.

He followed her finger and his eyes opened so wide it was almost comical. "That's for us?"

"All for you," I assured him. "Let's just say there were extra donations after your bravery last night."

We'd gotten almost as much in one-off donations as we had from the auction. Davy was the star of the night, and I was never, ever, going to tell him that.

A huge donation had come from my father for saving his little girl, but he'd asked me to keep it anonymous.

"It won't last forever," I warned. "You'll need to work out a funding program. But you can rebuild Momma's sanctuary."

The Jenner siblings stared at me, both with shining eyes, then Davy enfolded Robyn in his arms.

"I wish she was here to see it," he whispered.

Robyn nodded and sniffed. "She'd have been so proud of you last night."

I waited for Davy to say it was nothing or some other false modesty. But he just said, "She would have expected it. Elle's our family."

Now it was my turn for tears in my eyes.

Justin nudged my arm. "Don't lose these guys, boss. I like them. Also Robyn is the best assistant I've ever had."

I rolled my eyes. "Nice to see where your priorities lie."

We grinned at each other. We really were a perfect match in the office.

I looked over to see Davy and Robyn staring at us. They were obviously exhausted. "Want to go home now?"

Robyn sighed. "Yes, please. I don't mean to be rude, Elle, but I really hate it here. I want to be back on our farm."

Davy just nodded in agreement.

"The handcuffs are waiting on your call," Justin said. "Your hunky boyfriend insisted I call him as soon as you arrived, Robyn. He's probably pounding through the house as we speak."

At least that made Robyn smile. Sure enough, Griff appeared in under a moment and went straight over to Robyn.

"Are you all right," he asked, taking her hands.

"I am now you're here," Robyn said, and if her bottom lip quivered tremulously, she held her head high and expression fierce.

I could tell by Griff's proud expression that he loved his warrior woman. I was also sure they didn't care if anyone else was in the room.

I glanced at Davy to see his attention was fixed on me. When our gazes locked, he held out his hand and I went into his arms.

"Are you okay?" he queried. "You had a real scare last night."

"I will be." Somehow I didn't mind admitting to Davy that I wasn't there yet.

His arms were strong around me and he murmured that he would always be here for me.

Davy was so quiet as we drove to the airport, I looked over at him to check he was all right. Griff had warned me Davy might also struggle in the aftermath of the incident. He'd seemed fine, but I worried Davy was trying to hide his feelings instead of being the prickly, loving man I was used to.

I slid my hand into his. "You're quiet."

He hummed, then he smiled at me. "I was thinking about the animal sanctuary and what we could do to make it better than before."

I chuckled, relieved and feeling slightly foolish. I'd been so busy worrying about him, it hadn't occurred to me he was already thinking ahead.

He raised an eyebrow. "What did you think was the matter?"

I could have obfuscated, but instead I told him the truth. "I was worried you were thinking about the auction."

"Whitely?" At my nod, he sighed. "I have thought about him. I haven't slept much since then."

The confession made me feel better because neither had I.

"Don't take this the wrong way, Elle, but I keep thinking about all the other Whitelys who've suffered like they did." He held up his hand, thinking I was going to protest, but I said nothing, wanting to see where he led with this. "I don't think your family can be blamed for Mrs. Whitely's death, but guys like him—like me— spend a lot of time thinking about what happened and where it went wrong. Where they could have saved their wife or momma."

"You've been thinking about this too," I said.

He held onto my hand tighter as he gazed out of the window. "You could have been killed because he'd twisted it up in his mind and that scares me. Guys like Whitely need help."

"They do," I agreed. "And I'm looking into that right now."

Then he turned to study me. "You are?"

I stared at our joined hands, both tanned from years working in the sun. "Mr. Whitely is facing a long jail sentence because no one made a call just asking how he was. Not his family. Not his employer. I want to know how we can change that."

"Thank you." He kissed my knuckles. "Justin told me you've hired a lawyer for him."

"He needs help, not twenty-five to life."

"Do you think he'll stay out of jail?"

I sighed. "No, but the lawyer might be able to get the sentence reduced."

"You're a kind soul, Elle."

I leaned against him. "I had a good teacher."

Robyn and Griff walked together; his head bowed as if he were listening to what she had to say.

I watched Davy walk away to the plane. He turned to look at me and waved his hand. He went to go up the steps, stopped, then strode over to me. Not seeming to care about the men around me, he put his hand around my neck and kissed me. When he pulled back, his smile was soft.

"I love you, Elle. Not just for helping us with the auction. But because I've never stopped loving you."

Then he jogged back to the plane before I could respond and this time he didn't look back.

Chapter 19

Davy

I found Griff on the stoop early one morning a week after the auction. "Uh, Griff. I didn't expect to see you here. Is Elle with you?" I asked hopefully, even though the yard was obviously empty apart from him.

Griff got to his feet and stretched. The guy was huge. If I didn't like him I'd have been intimidated by his size.

"She tried to make it down, but her job is crazy," he said.

I hesitated, but then I had to ask, "Is Elle okay?"

Elle had been avoiding my calls since the auction. I wasn't sure what I'd done to upset her, but aside from a voicemail telling me she was busy, I hadn't heard from her.

I caught Griff's unhappy expression. "What's wrong with her?" I demanded.

"Can we do this over coffee," he asked. "It's cold out here."

"You could have knocked," I pointed out.

"I didn't want to wake you up."

I laughed. "Griff, we ain't city folk. We've been up for hours. Robyn is working in the office." I saw his eyes light up. "Go say hello to her and I'll put on another pot of coffee."

Saying hello took a while and by the time he returned I was getting impatient.

Griff pinked when I looked pointedly at the clock. "Sorry. I miss her, you know?"

I did know. I missed Elle so much it hurt.

"Tell me what's wrong with Elle," I demanded as he sat down and took the cup I offered him. He wrapped his hands around the cup and took a long slurp before he spoke.

"She's struggling with the incident with the gunman. This is the first time Elsa's come face-to-face with the reality of being a Ralston in the public face."

I frowned. "I don't understand. She's always been a Ralston."

"But there are Ralstons...and Ralstons." Griff almost drawled the words.

I'd heard that before. I wasn't sure where. Maybe Elle said it to me when we were kids.

Griff leaned back in his seat. "Before her grandfather died, Elsa could do what she liked, go where she liked, and run her own business with no interference. Well, *minimal* interference. She wasn't on the radar. There were other members of the family higher up the pecking order than she was."

"But once he made her the face of the Ralston's she became top of the pecking order," I hazarded.

Griff threw back the coffee and held up his cup to be refilled which I did. "Yeah. You don't live in Boston, so you don't see how people react to her. But Elsa Ralston is about as top of the tree as you can get. She's the wealthiest woman in Boston."

I could tell he'd never lived around here. After all, her family owned everything around here. I understood what he was trying to tell me. But why was she bothering with a poor farmer like me?

He looked up. "Don't do this to yourself, man. Elsa loves you and you're the closest thing to family she ever had."

My poker face obviously needed work.

"She has a family," I pointed out.

"One with no expectations. The Ralstons always have expectations."

I furrowed my brow. "That's very blunt. Don't you work for them?"

Griff shook his head. "I'm assigned to Elsa's protection detail, but I work for a company called Silver Cross. Although I've worked with the Ralston assignment for years, assigned to different members of the family. Old man Ralston helped me at a bad time."

"So now Elsa has discovered there's a world of difference between being Elle Ralston, landscape gardener, and Elsa Ralston, billionairess," I surmised.

"To be blunt, Elsa didn't take my team seriously. She calls us her handcuffs as if we're the ones restricting her movements."

I gave an understanding nod. "Whereas you're the ones making sure she *can* move."

"I know it's hard for someone to adapt to their change in circumstances." Griff grimaced. "I know that better than most people. But she has to understand her new position comes with responsibilities."

"So why are you here? Shouldn't you be protecting her?" I asked, almost angry he'd left her alone just so he could spend time with his girlfriend.

"Down, boy," he said, obviously reading my thoughts. "I'd already booked this time off as vacation before I met Robyn, and Elle's being protected by my team, led by my deputy. They're the best. I trained them."

No false modesty there then.

"Why is she avoiding me?" I asked.

"She's scared," Griff said.

"Scared of another attempt on her life?"

"Elsa is scared of you rejecting her," he said, and his voice was oddly gentle.

"Me?" I blinked at him, shocked.

"You. She's spent all this time trying to show you she's plain old Elle and really she's Elsa with a lot of Elle trying to get out."

"She's trying to avoid me because she thinks I might reject her?"

"That's what I just said."

I stared at Griff. "That's stupid."

"So what are you going to do about it?"

"He's going to get on that nice plane and fly to Boston and convince her that's she's wrong," Robyn said as she walked into the kitchen. She poured herself a cup of coffee and sat down at the table to look at us. She was mainly pretending not to stare at Griff, but as he was doing the same thing...it was painful to watch.

"I can't do that," I objected.

"Why not?" she asked.

"Because I'd have to go to Boston. I've been there twice this year and that's two times too many."

Robyn rolled her eyes at me. "If you're going to be Elsa Ralston's plus one, you'll be flying to Boston on a frequent basis."

I choked on my coffee. I was too busy coughing and spluttering to respond, but finally I managed to gasp out, "Plus one. What are you talking about?"

"You're her boyfriend. She goes to galas. You'll be her plus one."

I stared at her in horror. "I can't do that. Just no. Me. At a gala."

"You managed last week," she pointed out.

"Because it was for the sanctuary. I'm not going to do it voluntarily."

Robyn shrugged as if it were no big deal. "I guess there are plenty of eligible men to escort Elsa to a gala." At my growl she opened her eyes wide. "Make up your mind, big brother. You can't have it both ways."

"Sorry to interrupt your freak-out on something that hasn't happened," Griff said, "but are you going to Boston or not? Because I'll need to organize the plane."

They both stared at me. I stared back. There really was only one answer. "I guess I'm going." I wasn't going to let my Elle avoid me when what she really needed was a hug.

Robyn gave me a huge smile. "You made the right choice."

"I hope so," I muttered, "or I'm never leaving this farm again."

The pilot and copilot of the plane greeted me with smiles and called me sir and settled me in a huge leather chair. I had a coke and chips before we took off. They were so kind to me, and I felt bad because I was just a nobody. They laughed when I said that.

The copilot laughed. "You're our passenger and that makes you the most important person on the plane. Apart from him." He pointed to the pilot. "We need him."

"You can fly the plane as well as I can," the pilot pointed out.

I cocked my head. "So both of you are more important than me?" I chuckled and relaxed as they both laughed.

"I guess so," the copilot agreed. "But you have fun anyway."

I relaxed then and let them deal with the important work while I sat back and wondered what the heck I was going to say to Elle.

Griff had arranged my car to Ralston House. When they pulled up in front of the huge entrance, I was tempted to ask them to take me straight back to the plane, but I took a deep breath and headed for the front door. A thin man with wispy hair I thought I recognized opened the door. "Mr. Jenner?"

"Uh...yes?"

"My name is Marsden. We met at the Ralston

auction. The first one.”

I nodded and held out my hand. I remembered him.

He looked surprised, and then he shook my hand. “It’s good to see you again. I’ll take you to Ms. Ralston.”

I kept my shoulders back and head held high as we walked across the hallway. The place still intimidated me.

He led me through a complex maze which I realized were offices rather than the residential part of the house. Then he knocked and opened the door.

“Mr. Jenner to see Ms. Ralston.”

It was at this point I realized I’d come all this way without even checking to see if Elle would be here.

Marsden guided me in and shut the door behind me, leaving me facing one man who looked surprised and confused.

“David, it’s good to see you. Is Elsa expecting you?” Justin said.

I felt even more foolish. “No. I guess I should have made an appointment.”

Justin smiled at me. “Go on in. You’re probably the only person she wants to see right now.”

I wasn’t sure about that, but I took him at his word. I opened the door to her office to find Elle, her face buried in her arms. I studied her for a moment, not sure if she was napping or not.

“Elle?”

Her head shot up. I almost laughed at her wide eyes and parted lips, her red hair wild. This was my Elle, not Elsa, even if she was dressed in a designer suit.

"Davy, what are you doing here?"

"You're avoiding me. I came to find out why."

"I'm not avoiding you."

"Yeah, you are." I walked over to the desk and sat down in the chair in front of it. "You're not taking my calls. Griff says—"

She groaned. "Don't tell me he called you."

"Worse. He took your plane and came to find me."

"I'm going to have to hide the plane," she muttered.

I leaned forward. "What have I done wrong, Elle?"

"You stepped in front of a man pointing a gun at me."

She got to her feet and started to pace around the room. I could see she was angry. I wasn't sure if she was angry at me or herself. Maybe a little of both.

"I wasn't going to let him shoot you. He was upset, not dangerous. I wanted to distract him long enough for Griff to do his thing."

"He could have killed you," she yelled.

I knew that. I'd dreamed about it. "I'd do the same thing in a heartbeat. To protect you from anger."

"He could have shot you," she whispered, "and I'd never have forgiven myself."

I pulled Elle into my arms, and we sat down on the couch. "I missed you," I whispered into her fragrant bright hair. "Don't ever do that to me again."

"I was scared you'd send me away for putting you and Robyn in danger," she admitted, her fingers curling around the collar of my jacket.

Griff was very perceptive.

"Never," I promised. "I won't ever send you away. You're part of my heart, my home." I took her hand and placed it over my heart to show her. I covered her delicate hand with my own.

"You promise?"

"I promise."

"Your hands are so soft now," I murmured.

She sighed. "I'm so tired of being Elsa. I want to go back to my days digging ponds and hauling rocks. I want to be Elle."

That was more my Elle than the woman dressed in midnight blue silk would ever be. "You'll always be Elle to me. Come home with me."

"I need to work on the plane."

"You can work as much as you need to, as long as you're with me," I assured her, and she gave me a tender smile.

Then I heard voices outside the office.

Elle sighed again and pulled away from me. "Brace yourself," she muttered.

Chapter 20

Elle

I was glad Davy was by my side as I rose to face Mom and Dad as they entered the room, dressed in Armani suits, as though they just left a boardroom rather than our country club. I could tell Mom wasn't happy to find Davy with me, but I didn't care.

"Mom. Dad."

Mom scowled at me. "What's that man doing here?"

Davy stiffened beside me at her tone. His momma would never have spoken about me like that. I brushed the back of his hand with mine to comfort him and glared at my mother. She didn't get to be rude to the man I loved.

"David—you remember the man who saved me, don't you—came to make sure I was all right after the incident."

My tone dripped with sarcasm. I wanted to air quote the word. The 'incident' is how my parents described it, as if it were a minor thing. As if nearly being abducted was something that happened every day.

My father had the grace to look embarrassed, but my mother's stony expression didn't change one iota. I was aware of my father pleading with his eyes not to make this a big deal, but my patience was at an end.

I slipped my hand into Davy's and leaned against him. Mom's gaze snapped to our joined hands. I sighed. I remembered Lily telling me about her confrontation with her mother over Greg. Why couldn't they accept our choices? I held Davy's hand and sat down, tugging me down with him.

"Davy and I are going back to the farm this evening. We have a few issues to clear up from the auction and getting the sanctuary ready," I said.

Rebuilding the sanctuary was already well underway thanks to the outstanding help from Greg and Griff. But my parents didn't need to know this. I just needed to get away from here and take a deep breath.

"You have the Mayfield Gala on Saturday," Mom said. "Jeremy Forrester is escorting you."

I saw the smug look she flashed at Davy. Fortunately I'd told Davy about the gala weeks ago and my mom's marital aspirations with Jeremy Forrester. He'd heard enough about the man from Lily and Greg. I saw Mom narrow her eyes at Davy's lack of response.

"I'll be there," I assured her. "Valerie Crenshaw is delivering my dress tomorrow. Justin has arranged for the rubies to be delivered from the bank. The handcuffs have been alerted."

Mom looked disappointed. I could see she wanted something to complain about.

I looked at Davy and he nodded. He was as

ready as me to get this discussion over and done with. I held his hand tighter and looked at my parents. "There's something Davy and I need to know. Mom, did you tell Grandfather to threaten Davy's family if we continued to see each other?"

I saw the confusion in my father's eyes, but more importantly, I saw the flash of fear in Mom's eyes and knew it was true. She'd never expected that piece of information to come to light.

"Jennifer," Dad said slowly, "is this true? Was it you, not Pops, who wanted Davy out of Elsa's life?"

She turned to face him and flinched at his expression. "He and I decided it together, Edward. It was the right thing to do. Elsa would have been stuck on that silly farm, pregnant at eighteen. Pops wanted her to run the company. She was only sixteen. It didn't matter." Mom spoke about me as if I wasn't sitting in front of her.

Davy's hand strangled mine, but I didn't pull away. Instead I gave him the strength he needed.

"You told Granddad exactly how to manipulate Davy, because you knew how much he loved his family," I stated, wanting this out in the open.

"He had a choice of you or his family," she said dismissively. "He chose his family."

"Because Ralston told me he'd force my family out of the farm," Davy snarled. "I wanted to marry Elle and he said he'd throw us out if I laid a finger on her."

Even though I'd heard it before, it still made me flinch.

My dad stared at Mom as if he couldn't believe what he'd just heard. Had he really been ignorant all these years? "You made Pops threaten the Jenners?"

"It was for her own good," Jennifer insisted. "She was Elsa Ralston. They weren't good enough for her."

"Elle loved Davy. You saw what it did when Davy walked away. It nearly destroyed her. Skip was my fishing buddy. He refused to talk to me again. You should have told me."

I always forgot how much our fathers had liked each other. No matter the difference in their bank accounts, they were both simple men who liked the land and loved fishing. Dad was like me and retreated to Black Feather farm to clear his head. The Jenners had always welcomed him. It wasn't only me who'd lost someone. My father had lost his best friend. So many people hurt. For what? Status?

Jennifer shrugged. "She was sixteen. Plenty of time to make a suitable match."

"We nearly lost her, Jennifer. If Pops hadn't died, she would never have come back from Ohio. I can't believe you conspired with my father."

Dad stood up and looked at me. No, he was focused on Davy. He walked over and held out his hand. "I'm sorry, son. You didn't deserve that. I'd never have allowed the Ralstons to throw you out of the farm."

Davy got to his feet and shook my father's hand. "Thank you, sir. That means a lot. My dad would have been pleased to know it wasn't you. He missed you too. And you are always welcome at the farm. Maybe we could go fishing together."

I swallowed back a lump when I saw my father's thrilled expression. The man who could have anything his heart desired, wanted nothing more than a few hours fishing with his old buddy's son.

I stood too, and when they were finished, hugged my father. He had been caught between a domineering father and a volatile wife. He and I were alike in many ways, both of us drawn to the Jenner family because of the peace they had offered us.

My father looked down at me. "Get out of here, kiddo. Justin and I can handle anything that happens for a couple of days."

I nodded. "But make sure he doesn't work 24/7. You have to force him to go home."

He grinned at me. "I will."

He kissed my cheek and shooed the two of us out of the room, without even acknowledging Mom was sitting there, still as a statue. Then he shut the door. I understood. He was going to talk to his wife, but he wouldn't do it in front of us. He had more respect for her than that.

I didn't want to fight with my mom, but it would take me a long time to forgive her for her machinations with my grandfather, and I wouldn't forget. Judging by Davy's fixed expression, nor would he.

The outer office was empty. Justin's tidy desk had just an open planner and his tablet. He didn't really need the planner as he had our schedules on the tablet, but he kept it for my parents.

"Listen." I took Davy's hand in mine. "Let me

talk to Justin, find my handcuffs, and get out of here."

He squinted at me. "Have you got the work you need to bring?"

"Justin can send it to me."

His relieved exhale told me exactly what I needed to know. He was as anxious to get out of here as I was.

At that point Justin walked into the room.

"Davy and I are going home for a couple of days," I told my wonderful assistant. "Dad says he liaise with you on anything important, but you can call me if you need to. Call me," I added, to make sure he understood.

It wasn't until I saw they were both staring at me I realized what I'd said.

I chewed on my bottom lip. "I'm sorry. That wasn't...I didn't mean—"

Davy squeezed my hand. "The farm is as much your home as mine."

And I knew he didn't mean financially.

"I'll call your protection detail," Justin said, picking up his phone. "Damon is in command today."

"Thanks, Justin." I felt the tension trickling out of me at the prospect of being on the plane soon.

"Do you need to pack?" Davy asked as Justin made the call.

I shook my head. "I left clothes in Robyn's closet."

Davy huffed. "Let's get outta here."

"I wish I didn't have to come back for the gala, but Mom would never forgive me if I missed it."

"Don't you have a stand-in for occasions like this?"

"Mom *is* the stand-in," I pointed out. "But she always tells me I'm the one people are there to see." I gave him a wry smile. "I wear the frocks and the jewels and smile, and I bring the Ralston bank account."

"So cynical for one so young," Justin cooed as he disconnected the call. He dissolved into chuckles at my glower.

"Careful, mister, or I'll make you wear the dress," I threatened.

Justin rolled his eyes. "I'd rock a long dress and a tiara. Tuxedos are so boring."

We both laughed as Davy blinked.

"He's not joking," I said to Davy. "I've seen the photos. Sadly, we have to be conventional at the Mayfield gala."

I ushered my poor bemused Davy out of my office to find Griff's second-in-command waiting for us by the door.

"The car is ready," he said. "I've organized the two SUVs."

The handcuffs had ramped up their security since the incident at the auction. I wasn't surprised we needed an extra vehicle.

I waited for him to give the signal it was clear, then Davy and I got into the back of the car. Davy exhaled in relief when we pulled away from the house.

"You hate it here, don't you," I teased.

Davy gave me a rueful grin. "Is it that obvious?"

"Just a bit."

"It's not my world. Even this car intimidates me," he confessed. "I miss my beat-up Ford."

"I used to feel the same way every time we visited my grandfather. You remember our house. It wasn't that special. We didn't live the life of a Ralston until my grandmother died. My mom thought she was marrying into the Ralston empire and then discovered my dad never wanted to be part of the family. I wasn't the only one who ran away."

"I always liked your dad," Davy said.

I noticed he didn't extend the same courtesy to my mother.

"Dad is a very good businessman. Better than I'll ever be. He has an eye that comes from his father."

"So why did your grandfather make you the face?"

"To spite my father for not wanting to work in the family firm."

Davy wrinkled his brow. "Wouldn't he have done better to give the empire to another relative?"

"He wouldn't do that. He would only give it to one of his direct line. You've heard about the Ralstons born on the wrong side of the tracks, like Marisa Rosen's family?"

Davy nodded.

"The empire had to go to Dad or me. Granddad bypassed my father and gave everything to me, to spite his son. He knew Dad wouldn't let me sink. He'd have to get involved."

"Your family are crazy, scary people."

"And yet you still want to know me." I beamed at him.

"You are different. You make the world a better place," he assured me.

I sighed as Davy put his arms around my shoulders. "That was the right thing to say." I wriggled closer to him and rested my head against his chest. "You make the world a better place too, Davy Jenner."

Chapter 21
Davy

I was in the yard with Griff, discussing the opening day of the sanctuary and who we were going to invite. We had our local celebrities like the mayor and the sheriff. We'd already thought about asking the local shelters too. Elle had promised to bring people from Boston who'd contributed to the auction, plus Greg's grandmother, Marisa. The only person I really wanted there was my sweet momma. I hoped she was happy as she looked down at us.

"Are you expecting a visitor?" Griff said, looking over my shoulder and distracting me from my wistful thoughts.

"Not today." I turned to see a dust cloud making its way down the drive. As it drew closer, I recognized the pick-up truck. "That's Charlie Reedham."

Griff obviously heard my grim tone. "The guy who threatened you before?"

"The neighbor, yeah. He's left us alone since then. What does he want now?"

I folded my arms across my chest and waited for the vehicle to stop. Reedham got out of the truck. His expression changed when he spotted the huge man at my side. He'd clearly expected me to be alone. Easier to threaten, I guess. Griff was a silent sentinel, and it felt good to have his support. I knew the rest of the handcuffs would be somewhere out of sight, ready to act if necessary.

Reedham nodded at me. "Jenner."

"What do you want, Reedham?" I said, my tone flat and unfriendly.

"You haven't responded to my offer."

"I did. I said no. This is Jenner land."

Reedham's scowl deepened. "It's a fair offer."

"Fair? It's worth one tenth of the value of the farm," I said, my voice rising in anger.

Reedham just shrugged. "As I said, fair. Your farm isn't worth the paper it's written on. Your girlfriend saved you this time. She ain't gonna keep doing it. She's a Ralston. She ain't gonna pour good money after bad."

He put his finger on my greatest fear. When would Elle wake up to the fact Black Feather farm was a money pit? The sanctuary was going to eat money, not provide an income. Even with the auction the money would run out sooner or later.

Reedham's eyes narrowed, and he nodded in grim satisfaction. I'd obviously not been as good as I thought at hiding my emotions. "Take the offer."

"The answer's still no," I said.

"And you're wrong, Mr. Reedham."

I turned to see Elle glowering at the man, her head held high. Despite the casual clothes she wore, she was all Elsa Ralston.

Reedham turned to study her, and his lip curled. I was ready to punch him for dismissing her like that, but I felt a quick touch on my back. Griff was telling me to calm down.

"Your grandfather would know better, little lady. You should listen to the men," Reedham sneered.

Elle looked down at him. If she'd aimed that look my way, I'd have shriveled into dust. Sadly, Reedham stayed intact.

"I am," she said, and she smiled at me.

My heart melted again. I was never going to let this strong, fierce woman out of my life.

"I'm going to the Ralston board," Reedham snarled. "It don't matter who you send after me. I know these men and they won't let you do this."

"I know them too," she pointed out. Elle leaned on the railing and fixed him with an icy gaze. "Let me make one thing clear, Reedham. I could *personally* buy your ranch out like that." Elle snapped her fingers. "And still not break into a sweat. *You* will never get your hands on the Jenners' farm."

Reedham's face went an ugly shade of red. He was furious at the power this young woman had. I tensed, worried he was going to launch himself at Elle—or worse. I was too far away to protect her this time, as was Griff.

"You'll regret this, missy."

Before I could yell at him, Griff calmly walked around me and put himself between Reedham and Elle. I breathed a little easier.

Griff folded his arms across his chest, emphasizing just how big his muscles were, and fixed his gaze on Reedham. "Don't even think about it, Reedham. You insult my employers and I'll take you down in one move."

Reedham growled and turned to snarl at me. "They won't be here forever. You wait."

I raised an eyebrow. "Is that a threat, Reedham?"

"It's a promise, Jenner. You're finished here."

Reedham threw himself into his vehicle and drove away, taking out a row of trash cans in the process.

"I don't think that's the last you're going to hear of him," Griff muttered.

I was afraid he was right, but there was one thing I needed to settle first. I raised an eyebrow at him. "Employ-*ers*?"

He rolled his eyes. "You know what I mean."

Elle walked down the stoop, a mischievous grin playing about her lips. "Is there something you need to tell me, Griff?"

To his obvious relief, four black-clad men appeared from around the barns, holstering their weapons. Charlie Reedham didn't know how lucky he was. If he'd tried to attack Elle, he might not have lived through the encounter.

"Contact Damon," Griff said to one of the men. "Reedham threatened Elsa. He needs further investigation."

"I should make a few calls too before Mr. Reedham gets the chance to cause more trouble," Elle said.

What was I supposed to do? Feed the chickens and try not to imagine what stunt Reedham might pull next?

I studied Elle. "Did you just threaten to buy him out like that?" I snapped my fingers as she had.

Elle shrugged. "Justin did some investigation into his finances. Mr. Reedham wants to sell to a developer for rezoning as housing. But he promised your farm to sweeten the deal."

I frowned. "So he doesn't want to keep the ranch?"

"Reedham has other plans."

She didn't say what they were, and I didn't ask, too focused on the idea of losing the fine old ranch neighboring ours. I'd always told my daddy we would buy that ranch one day.

I shook my head, feeling inadequate. "I'm just a farmer."

Elle jogged down the stoop to put her arms around me. "And that's what I love about you, Davy. Guys like Reedham are always out for the big bucks. They don't care about this land. You do."

I wrapped my arms about her and rested my head on her chin. She always knew how to make me feel better. Griff and the other men faded away, leaving us alone in the yard.

"I've got to go home tomorrow," she said, sounding less than enthusiastic.

I grimaced at the thought. Two days hadn't been nearly long enough. "Don't remind me."

She raised her head and looked at me. "One last sunrise at the creek before I go home?"

I smiled at her and brushed a kiss over her lips. "I was gonna drag you out of bed for that."

Elle reached up and cupped my jaw and I leaned into her caress. "You're all scratchy."

I rasped my chin against her palm. I hadn't shaved that morning. "I could grow a big beard."

She laughed, knowing as well as I did that I couldn't grow a decent beard. I took after my dad. Neither of us had been able to grow a beard to save our lives. Momma had come from a family of men with bushy beards and had been disappointed at our lack of hirsuteness.

"I could buy you a fake beard," Elle suggested.

"Make sure it matches my hair color."

She smiled at me. "A bright red beard. Leave it with me. I'll get Justin to order it along with the stationery."

Then the smile slipped from her face, and she leaned against me again. I held her tight.

"I love you, Elle," I whispered. "I'll never let that man hurt you."

I didn't say which man. It could be any man. If I had the chance, I'd stand between her and the rest of the world.

"Likewise," she murmured. "He'll never get a chance to hurt you or the farm."

I held her close and hoped we could both keep our promises.

I smiled as Elle shuffled into the kitchen the next morning, her eyes still half-closed. She wore an old pair of pajama bottoms, and a faded hoody I was sure was one of mine. Her feet were bare, just peeping out from the pajama pants. I could see pale pink nail polish on her toes.

Bailey rushed over to greet her. She patted his head, not even opening her eyes, and headed for the table.

"Good morning," I said cheerfully.

She grunted at me as she sat down.

"Nice." I grinned. I never knew which Elle I was going to find in the morning.

"Coffee?"

Knowing I wasn't going to get any more from her until she was caffeinated, I poured a cup of the fragrant brew and topped it off with creamer, then I eased it into her hands.

I poured my own cup and sat opposite her. "Did you sleep?"

"Not really. I got a call and had to work late." She rested her elbow on the table and propped her chin up with her hand, her eyes still hooded. "Then when I did sleep it was full of bad dreams."

"The incident?"

Elle gave a wry smile. "Even you call it the incident."

"It makes it easier to think about," I admitted. I still went cold every time I thought about the guy waving the gun at Elle.

"I guess it does," she said softly. "I kept dreaming that he fired the gun and didn't miss."

"You dreamed he hit me?"

She nodded. "Over and over. It's been like that every night. I kneel by your body and beg you to stay with me. Pray that you're alive. I always wake up before I get an answer."

I went a little cold. I'd had those dreams too, except mine were not reaching Elle in time.

I stroked the back of her hand. "What can I do to reassure you I'm safe?"

"Come into my dreams and tell me you're alive?"

"I'll do that," I promised.

She gave me that tender smile and my heart skipped a beat.

I made toast and we drank a second cup of coffee before we headed to the barn. The horses greeted us with enthusiasm and before long, we were riding out in the deep blue of the pre-dawn light. We talked about everything and nothing as we rode toward the creek, but finally I asked the question I needed to know.

"When will you be back?" I asked.

She sighed. "I don't know. The mergers are taking all my attention. I have to be there."

It was always going to be like this. Two days of her by my side and then she'd be gone for weeks.

I watched the sunlight bathe Elle's face as she closed her eyes. It was now or never. This was the last morning and if I missed this opportunity, who knew when I would see her again. I fumbled in my pocket. "Elle."

Elle opened her eyes and smiled at me. "Yes?"

I went down on one knee and took her hand with my free one. She stared at me, obviously shocked.

"Will you marry me?" I asked.

Chapter 22

Elle

Davy stared up at me, looking determined and scared at the same time. "Will you marry me?"

He held out a small emerald-green jewelry box and flipped it open. I gasped as I saw the square cut emerald ring. I knew how precious this was. I had seen this ring on his momma's finger every day I'd known her. It had been her momma's ring, and it was worn and well-loved.

"Oh, Davy." I gasped. Then I bit my lip and nodded. "Yes. Yes. Yes."

Maybe that was a little over the top, but it was enough to erase the fear from his expression. He got to his feet and took the ring out of the box. I stopped him, one hand over the ring.

"Davy, shouldn't this go to Robyn?"

He smiled and shook his head. "Robyn inherited Daddy's mom's rings. Momma always intended this to go to my bride."

He slipped the ring on my finger and if his hands were shaking, that was okay. Mine were too. It fitted perfectly. He kissed the ring and then the palm of my hand.

"It's beautiful," I murmured.

"I know you could afford the ring of your

dreams," he said.

I curled my fingers around his hands and held on tight. "This is the ring of my dreams from the man I love."

I had a safe full of precious stones back at Ralston House and more in the bank, and none of them meant as much to me as this well-worn, well-loved ring.

"Momma told me she wanted the ring for my bride, but she meant you," he said. "I'll show you the note she left me."

Tears prickled the back of my eyes. Even after her death Davy's momma still showed her love for me.

I rested my head on his chest, the ring on my hand over his heart, and listened to the sounds of the farm waking up in the distance. Davy's large hand cupped my head. I could have stayed listening to the comforting sound of his heartbeat all day, but I knew when he sighed it was time for reality to intrude.

I looked up at him. "Davy, can we get married here?"

He furrowed his brow. "On the farm?"

I shook my head. "I mean here, by the creek."

"Don't you want to get married in Boston?" He grinned as I shuddered. "I guess that's a no."

I took his hands in mine. This was a conversation we needed to have and now was as good a time as any. "The last couple of months have taught me that I don't need to be based in Boston. I thought I did. But I've spent weeks flying over the country. I think I've been in Boston twice.

I've spent more time here."

"What about your friends there?"

"I have one friend in Boston. Lily. Well, two if you count Greg." I wrinkled my brow. "Three, including his gran. Anyway, they're in Maine now, not Boston. And we can take the plane to see them. Greg loves coming here, you know that."

Greg had loved it so much; he'd made noises about buying a place here too. Lily, not so much, but she would do it for Greg. I'd already thought about suggesting we convert one of the barns as a guest residence for them, but baby steps.

I held his hands tighter. "I'm not a city girl, Davy. You know that. I'm not Elsa Ralston." I wrinkled my nose and he laughed. "I want to live here with you and Robyn and Griff. I don't even need to keep my handcuffs here as Griff is here too."

"And your parents?" he asked.

"Dad loves it here. Mom..." I sighed. Things were still fragile between us. I loved her dearly, but some things were hard to forgive. I knew how Lily felt now. "I'll visit Mom and do events and go shopping and all the things that Elsa Ralston is supposed to do. But I'll spend my nights here, sleeping next to you."

His smile was all I needed to see. I'd said the right thing.

"You do that," he said. "But if I think you're getting overtired with all the traveling I'll say so."

"You do that," I said, echoing him.

I rested my head on his chest for a moment. I wasn't ready to let him go yet. But the world had other ideas. My phone buzzed and so did Davy's. I pulled mine out.

"You've got to go?" Davy said.

"I have. The plane is waiting."

It was so unfair. He'd just asked me to be his wife. But I had an empire, and he had a farm to take care of. We both had responsibilities.

He gave me a boost onto Lemondrop's back. "If you're staying, I guess you need a horse of your own."

I nodded in agreement because we would never subject Peardrop to anything that frightened her. "We could look for new horses for you and Robyn too."

"I'll phone around. See what's available," he said.

We took a slow ride back to the house, neither of us wanting to part a moment sooner than we had to, but all too soon the house and barns came into view. Davy turned the horses out into the paddock with a promise he would love on them after he'd loved on his fiancée. This man could melt my heart.

Robyn took one look at us and squealed so loudly, Bailey started barking in confusion. Griff looked equally confused.

"Show me," she demanded.

I grinned at her and held out my left hand. She rushed over to study the ring as if it were the first time she'd seen it, rather than a ring she'd seen almost every day of her life.

"I'm missing something," Griff said.

Robyn looked over her shoulder. "Davy and

Elle just got engaged."

He got up from the table and came over to look at the ring. "How did you know?"

She rolled her eyes. "You can't see the huge dopey grins on their faces?"

"They always look like that when they're together," he grumbled.

I stared at Davy. He looked as bemused as me.

"When is the wedding?" Robyn asked.

"We haven't gotten that far yet," Davy said.

"Soon," I insisted. "And we're getting married by the creek."

Robyn gave me a sweet smile. "That's perfect." Then her smile dissolved into giggles. "Your mom's gonna be furious."

I groaned. "Don't remind me."

She would be so angry that I'd taken away her one chance to be mother of the bride.

Davy shrugged. "Why don't we have two weddings? The real one here and one for your family at the Ralston House so your mom gets her day."

"You'd do that for my mom?" How had I gotten so lucky?

He kissed my cheek. "I'd do it for you because you want to make your mom happy. And she deserves her day in the spotlight."

I beamed at him, and I swore Robyn sniffled.

I went to get my bag from Robyn's bedroom and returned to hear Davy saying, "And Griff too. If he's living here, he needs a horse."

It turned out Griff did not want a horse. I discovered my burly bodyguard was petrified of horses. I mean face go pale, hands shaking, petrified. Griff would face down a man with a gun, but horses made him shake. Robyn giggled but she hugged him tightly.

"I'll buy you a quad bike instead," I promised, and Griff brightened. I knew him well enough to know he would spend the flight home looking at which model to buy.

Davy eyed me speculatively.

"Yes, you can have a quad bike too," I assured him.

It turned out once Davy got over his hang-ups about me being a Ralston and ridiculously wealthy, he was happy to spend the money if it was something practical for the farm. He still resisted my attempts to buy him a bespoke tuxedo.

We walked out onto the verandah and Davy opened his arms. I stepped inside to be enfolded in his embrace. His tender kiss would have to keep me going until I returned. Inside the house, Robyn was saying goodbye to Griff. We would be back soon, but the separation was hard on all of us.

"You seem lost in thought," Davy said.

I gave him a wry smile. "You've given me a lot to think about."

"Are you worried about your parents?"

I shook my head. Then nodded ruefully. "They're going to insist on a prenuptial agreement."

He knit his brows. "Of course. I expected it."

"You don't mind?" I asked anxiously. We'd only just gotten engaged. I didn't want anything to jeopardize us.

"I expected it. You have a family empire to protect, Elle. Do you think it's a good idea?"

I nodded, relieved he'd taken the idea so calmly. "I think a prenup is a good thing. I would never do anything to endanger my family or businesses. But you and Robyn will never want for anything again. I promise you that."

Davy stroked my hair. "Your generous heart never fails to amaze me. But you've already given me everything I ever wanted."

I thought he meant the farm, but then he brushed his lips over my knuckles, and I realized he meant me.

I wanted to kiss him but sudden footsteps behind me made me look over my shoulder. Griff gave me an apologetic smile.

"Sorry, boss. We have to leave now."

I nodded and turned back to Davy. "Thank you for making me the happiest woman in the world."

"Will you wear the ring to the gala?" he asked.

I furrowed my brow. That was a question I hadn't expected.

"It won't go with the rubies," he continued.

"Why are you worrying about that?" I was so confused.

"You're going on a date," Davy said.

And now it was clear. Despite his calm demeanor when my mom tried to provoke him, Davy was worrying about Jeremy Forrester, my escort to the gala. For a moment I thought about inviting Davy to be my escort, but he would hate it and I would be worrying about him all evening. I sought for another way to reassure him.

I placed my hand over his heart. "I will never take this ring off my finger. The whole world will see you asked me to be your bride, including my mom and Jeremy. I'm yours, Davy Jenner, and you are mine." I didn't laugh at his insecurity. If he needed my reassurance that's what he'd get.

"I love you, Elle," he rumbled. "I never stopped loving you."

I stared up into his dark green eyes. "I want to grow old and gray with you," I assured him. "I want to have matching rocking chairs as we hold hands together."

"I'll make them for you," he promised.

Davy kissed me then and I didn't care who saw us. I needed to say goodbye to my fiancé.

Chapter 23

Davy

I missed my Elle so much. She agreed to marry me and then disappeared for weeks. Not sure what to do, I kept working on the farm, grateful we could make the repairs now we had the income.

Thanks to the regular visits from Greg and Griff, we had rebuilt the animal sanctuary bigger and better than it was before, and it was ready for the first occupants, but the opening had been postponed until after our wedding on my request. There were only so many things I could handle, and I knew the sanctuary would take all our time. Robyn had pouted but she'd understood.

That was the plan. But someone hadn't gotten the message.

Early one morning, Robyn and I were talking over breakfast as we usually did before she disappeared into the office, and I went to feed the critters.

A dog barked. Confused, I looked at Bailey. He was asleep in front of the stove. Maybe he'd barked in his sleep.

Another bark. Robyn blinked. "That's the phone for the sanctuary."

"You set the ringtone to bark?" I asked incredulously.

"It fits," she pouted.

We both stayed where we were as it barked again.

"One of us had better answer it," I suggested.

Robyn launched for the cell phone before I could get there.

"Hello, Susan Jenner Animal Sanctuary."

I watched her expression change from confusion to excitement to fear.

"Now? How many? Euthanized. No, no, you can't do that. We'll take them. We're ready."

I suddenly realized what she'd agreed to. "We're getting animals?"

What about the wedding? My plans?

Robyn flapped her hand at me to shut me up and continued to nod and say "Yes, yes." She disconnected the call and stared at me. "We need to collect three senior dogs this morning. A pitbull, a Labrador, and a chihuahua. They're going to be euthanized today if we don't."

I scowled. "We're going to be blackmailed into taking the dogs."

"Yep. We need to collect them this morning from the shelter." Robyn sounded ecstatic. "I've got to tell Griff."

I raised an eyebrow and she glowered at me, although it was spoiled by the huge grin that she couldn't hide.

"Oh hush," she scolded, although I hadn't said a word. "He wants to be involved. You know he does."

I grinned at her. "I can't believe you found a guy just like you."

"I know." She almost bounced on her seat. "Do you want to come with me to get the dogs?"

Silly question. There was no way I was missing out on this, even if it wrecked all my plans.

"I do. Give me an hour and I'll be ready."

"Thirty minutes and not a moment more," she said. She tapped her watch. "Shoo! The clock's ticking."

I ran out of the door. My sister had turned into a monster. Momma would have approved.

Thirty minutes later we were on the road to the shelter. It was two hours from the farm, and I don't think Robyn drew breath the entire way. We'd done our research and we knew senior dogs had little chance of being adopted from a high kill shelter. Momma had always wanted a place where a dog could live out its days as comfortably as possibly. Robyn and I were more prosaic but still we wanted to try to honor Momma's wishes.

The shelter was a cacophony of frantic barking as we entered the reception. A middle-aged woman with medium length ash-blonde hair behind the counter gave us a professional smile.

Robyn strode up to the counter. "We're from the Susan Jenner Animal Sanctuary. I'm Robyn Jenner. We're here to collect three dogs."

The professional smile turned into a genuine one. "I spoke to you earlier. I'm Sue Croft. Thanks for coming so promptly."

"You say the three dogs are seniors?" Robyn asked.

Sue nodded. "The pitty is twelve, the lab is ten,

and the chihuahua also around ten. They're in good health and very friendly, but they've been here too long."

She grimaced and I understood. They were taking up space for younger, more adoptable dogs. Well, that's what we were here for.

"I'll bring them out," Sue said.

She vanished into the back and Robyn turned to look at me.

"This is it, Davy."

I nodded, as excited and nervous as she was. Then a door opened, and three dogs scrambled through the door, dragging Sue after them. My heart softened at first glance. The three animals looked so beaten down, their ears flat and their expressions...I heard Robyn catch her breath.

Sue looked at us and sighed. "You're new to this, aren't you?"

Robyn nodded; her attention focused on the dogs.

"Each animal will break your heart," Sue advised. "But you'll learn."

"To harden your heart?" I queried.

She shook her head. "You get a bigger heart."

Damn, I wasn't going to get all sentimental in front of a stranger. I bent to greet the tan pitbull with a light gray muzzle who rushed to slobber over me, a huge smile on its face. The Labrador and the chihuahua were more wary, but they too said hello.

"The pitty is Bella, the lab is Miles, and the chihuahua is Gizmo."

We signed the papers, then we walked out into

the sunshine with our first residents. It was only as we reached the truck, we realized we didn't have any cages for them to ride in and we had no idea how the three dogs would manage in a vehicle.

I looked at Robyn. "We didn't work this one out, huh?"

"It's a learning curve," she said with beatific smile. "We'll get a new truck. I allowed for it in the plan."

The ride home was...interesting. Miles sat in the back, as far away from us as he could get. He was the most nervous of the three. Bella stuck her head between the two front seats and drooled on my shoulder most of the way, while Gizmo curled up in Robyn's lap. But none of them tried to eat us or the truck so I counted it as a win.

We arrived home and walked into the animal sanctuary. Each pen was spacious, with access to an outside run.

Robyn, who had Gizmo in her arms, looked at me. "Let's take them for a walk first."

I sighed. "They're not going to live in the house."

"I know," she said quietly. "But when was the last time they got to be free?"

She was right. What was the point of having this land if they were just caged all the time?

I unclipped Bella's and Miles's leashes. "Come on, guys, let's explore your new home."

We took them to the meadow. Bella was off like a shot. For the oldest dog she seemed to have boundless energy. Miles stood stock still, like he couldn't quite believe he was standing on grass again. Gizmo stayed close to Robyn but rolled ecstatically on his back.

I scratched Bella behind the ears, grinning as she wiggled her butt in glee. "You know now we've taken the first ones the phone won't stop ringing, don't you?"

"That's what we're here for. I know it's not what you wanted but we couldn't say no, could we," she pleaded.

I gave her a nod and her smile grew wide.

"When's Griff turning up?" I asked.

"Tonight." She didn't bother to deny her boyfriend would be here as soon as he could.

"I'll make up the beds in the bunkhouse."

Since Elle's bodyguards came here on the regular basis, I'd done my best to make the bunkhouse more comfortable. We'd cleaned it through and put in new mattresses and bedding. I'd found better furniture and the couches were almost new. I'd also installed a large TV which cost more than the furniture, but the guys were appreciative.

"Already done," Robyn said.

I snorted which startled Gizmo and made him cower. Robyn glared at me and bent to coo at Gizmo. He melted against her. I had a feeling Gizmo would become a part of the family.

Farm chores needed to be done. I whistled for Bailey. He'd been told to stay in the yard, but now he happily joined us. The three rescue dogs looked at him warily but none of them showed any aggression. I knew we weren't always going to be so lucky, but I was happy to give these dogs as much freedom as they could handle.

The thought of Griff arriving made me miss Elle again. Maybe I'd call her later.

"I'll sort out dinner," Robyn said. "Come on, Gizmo."

I shook my head as she wandered off with Gizmo in her arms, but as Bella and Miles followed Bailey and me, I couldn't say too much.

I spent the day trying to catch up with running the farm. Bella and Miles behaved impeccably, and they listened to me ramble on as I told them about Elle. Bailey had heard it all before, but the other two dogs at least pretended to listen. Eventually though I thought it was time to settle them in the pens.

We ambled back to the yard as a dust cloud barreled down the drive. I tensed, half-expecting Charlie Reedham to appear, which was ridiculous because I hadn't seen him in weeks. As the SUV drew up, I saw Griff driving with Greg sitting next to him. Greg hopped out almost before the vehicle ground to a halt.

I smirked at him. "You running away from real work again?"

Greg waved a dismissive hand. "You've got animals." He knelt as Bella rushed over to him to say hello. "What a gorgeous girl. What a gorgeous girl."

Bella wiggled her rear end and drooled in glee, rolling over onto her back for a belly rub and he obliged.

"You'll be there forever," I warned.

"And this is a problem?" Greg carried on loving

on Bella. He looked over at Miles who was hanging behind me. "Who's this guy?"

I patted the lab's head. "This is Miles. He's unsure about everything at the moment."

"Hey there, Miles." Greg didn't make any attempt to get nearer to the nervous dog, but his greeting was calm and friendly.

Griff got out of the SUV and Robyn came out with Gizmo in her arms. I watched the huge man melt as his girl and their new dog were enfolded in his embrace.

And then it was my turn to turn into a puddle of goo, because two women got out of the back of the SUV and one of them had flame-colored hair. I strode over to her and wrapped her in my arms. Her hands curled around my shirt and held on as I kissed her.

I raised my head and waited for Elle to open her eyes. "You didn't tell me you were coming," I chided gently.

Elle's smile chased away the lonely weeks without her. "I wanted to surprise you. Also Griff was unbearable the second he heard you had your first dogs."

"I heard that," Griff said without looking away from Robyn. He was busy petting Gizmo who wore a huge smile, his tongue out.

"I thought you might," Elle said. "Now introduce me to our new residents."

I wrapped my arm around her shoulders and pointed to Robyn. "The little chi is Gizmo. I don't think Robyn has put him down since he arrived. Bella is the pitbull. She's a lovebug. And Miles here is a gentleman, but he likes to take things easy."

To my surprise, Miles nudged Elle's hand. She petted him gently. I didn't try to do the same. I wanted Miles to relax in his own time.

Bailey watched us from the stoop. He was watchful but not worried by the new arrivals.

"Griff and I will feed the dogs," Robyn said.

Greg pouted but he got to his feet. Bella waited and then huffed and rolled over when Greg didn't resume the petting. She bounded over when Robyn called her.

Elle grinned at me. "What are the chances of your first residents actually sleeping in their pens?"

"They're staying in the pens," I said firmly. "The house is Bailey's territory." I looked at my sister. "Except perhaps Gizmo. I think he's found his forever home."

Elle nuzzled into me. "Your sanctuary's first success."

I kissed the top of her head. "I think that's stretching it a bit."

"Take your successes where you can find them," she assured me and held me tight.

Chapter 24

Elle

It was late Monday morning, and I'd been working for six hours already. The figures weren't becoming clearer no matter how long I stared at them. I'd insisted on receiving the quarterly figures, so it was my own fault. But I was starting to feel trapped in my office. It was as if every company we owned decided to have issues just to thwart my plans.

I longed to be riding Lemondrop on Black Feather farm. The visit to meet the new residents of the sanctuary seemed like a distant memory, although Davy kept me supplied with videos of him with Bella and Miles, and several other dogs who'd moved in. I was supposed to be getting married in three weeks, but it was looking increasingly unlikely I'd be able to spare the time for my own wedding. I wasn't looking forward to having *that* conversation with Davy.

I looked up at the knock on the office door. I was grateful for any distraction from the company accounts.

Justin grinned at me. I noticed the pale yellow of his dress shirt matched the stripe on his tie. He always insisted on being formally dressed no matter how much I insisted he could dress down. I found myself wearing smarter clothes in response. Was this a ploy engineered by my mother to get me out of jeans?

"I know you said you didn't want to be disturbed but you have a visitor," Justin said.

I grimaced. "If it's from my mother about another dress fitting, tell her I've been kidnapped and taken to the south of France and I'm never coming back."

"It's not Mrs. Ralston," he assured me, and he almost managed to hold back the smirk.

I sighed and stared at the accounts once more. I should really focus on them, but I knew Justin wouldn't have disturbed me unless it was important. He was a very efficient guard dog.

"Who is it?" I asked.

Justin stepped back and Davy walked in, dressed in a new plaid shirt and Wranglers and wearing a huge grin on his face.

My jaw dropped. "Davy, what are you doing here?"

"I decided if my fiancée wouldn't come to me, I'd come to my fiancée." He held out his arms and I was out of my seat in an instant.

"I can't believe you're here again." I held him so tightly I swear I heard the air leave his lungs. "You don't know how much I need this."

"I do too," he assured me in a rumble above my head.

I stayed where I was, my head resting on his chest, inhaling his scent. But finally I looked up. "Why are you here? What about the farm and the sanctuary?"

"Griff is there to help Robyn."

I wrinkled my brow. "Griff is at the farm?"

"Griff is on vacation."

"He is?"

That was embarrassing. I hadn't even noticed he'd left. But then I hadn't gone anywhere in weeks. I'd been so busy working so I could take time away for my wedding, I hadn't needed the handcuffs.

"I thought I'd find my errant fiancée. Phone calls are not the same," Davy admitted. He was trying to be nice, but I could hear the hurt note he was trying to hide.

"I'm sorry, Davy. I never intended to stay away so long." I knuckled my eyes. "When was the last time I saw you?"

"Six weeks ago."

"This job is sucking the life from me," I muttered. I couldn't remember if it were six hours or six years ago. The only thing I'd focused on was the next problem.

Davy ran his hand over my hair. "You need a sunrise by the creek."

I could think of nothing better, but I had responsibilities.

"Maybe I could show you around Boston," I suggested. Surely I could squeeze that in. I could work through the night if necessary.

"I'd like that."

I grinned at his fake enthusiasm. "What you really want to do is kidnap me and run back to the plane, don't you?"

"Is it that obvious?"

I smirked at him. "It's okay, Davy. You're never going to be a city boy." I saw his shudder just at the thought and my smile grew wider

"What do you need to do to escape from your office?" he asked.

"I'm looking at the quarterly figures for each company. We're showing a decrease and I don't know why."

"Have you talked to the CEO or VP or whoever runs each company? Or your financial director? They must be able to explain the fluctuations."

I stared at him. "Uh...no. I thought I could work it out myself. I hate having to continually ask questions."

"That's how you're going to learn," Davy said, and I felt foolish. I'd been so determined to learn everything myself I forgot that each company had a wealth of experience.

Davy walked to the door, and I heard him talking to Justin. The next thing the phone on my desk trilled. I picked it up.

"It's Patrick Hinton for you," Justin said.

I took a deep breath. Patrick Hinton had been the financial director for Ralston longer than I'd been alive. I'd been foolish to ignore him.

"Elsa. It's good to hear from you," he said cheerfully. "I'd been wondering when you were going to call me."

I gave a resigned sigh. "Hi, Uncle Pat. How's Aunt Rosa?"

He was also my uncle by marriage. Aunt Rosa was my dad's sister. I was never going to live this down.

"She's fine. Nagging me to lose weight. The woman never gives up. You think she'd have learned after thirty-five years of marriage. Now, let's talk figures."

An hour later I staggered out of my office, with all the information I needed. I discovered Davy reading a magazine on yachting of all things.

Justin looked up from his tablet. "All good?"

"The empire is not about to collapse." I rubbed my temples in an effort to relieve the headache I could feel brewing there.

Davy dragged his attention away from the ten-million-dollar yachts and smiled at me. "That's good."

"Uncle Pat pointed out I should have called him sooner."

Davy didn't react to me calling the Financial Director Uncle Pat so I assumed Justin had given him that tidbit of information. "Sometimes you need an outsider to suggest your next move."

His warm smile told me that was exactly what I'd done for him. I returned his smile, and my day felt a little better.

"I'll call you next time I'm stuck," I assured him. "In fact, I'm going to call you with all my business problems." I laughed at Davy's expression of horror.

"That would be the quickest way for your empire to collapse," he said.

Justin looked at his watch. "You've got forty-eight hours until your next meeting, Elsa. You haven't taken a break in weeks. Why don't you go to the farm? I'll call you if the bottom drops out of the market between now and Wednesday."

That sounded wonderful. I looked at Davy. "Would you mind delaying your trip around Boston for a while?"

"I think I can handle it," he rumbled as he got to his feet. "You've got my number, Justin. Call me if you want to discuss it further."

I looked between my fiancé and my assistant, and raised an eyebrow. "Is there something I should know?"

"No," Davy assured me. "Nothing you have to worry about."

"Why doesn't that reassure me?" I grumbled.

"I have no idea. Are you ready to go?" he asked.

I was obviously not going to get anything out of either of them. "I just need to clear my desk. The plane—"

"Is fueled and ready for departure," Justin said. "And the SUV is waiting at the other end. Security is downstairs waiting for you. I'll clear your desk."

"Don't ever leave me," I said to him.

"Why would I do that?" Justin sounded like I'd just suggested something stupid.

"Ready to go?" Davy asked hopefully.

I smiled at him and held out my hand. "Ready to go."

As we headed to the car, I said, "I found out why Justin left Diana Duchamp's employ."

"Oh?"

"He didn't like the way she tried to break up Greg and Lily. He thought it was cruel."

"He left the job for that?" Davy sounded dubious.

"I think everyone has a breaking point. He reached his. He also knew he could walk into any job. Justin isn't stupid."

I was just the lucky one who got him, thanks to Lily.

As the plane taxied to a halt, I heard Davy's phone buzz. He pulled it out to look at the screen. "It's Robyn. She wants me to call."

He hit the button. "Hey, Robyn, we've just landed. What's up?"

I saw the color drain from his face. "What's happened?" I asked. "Is Robyn all right?"

Davy hit the speaker. "Elle's here too. Tell her what you just said."

"Someone tried to set fire to the animal sanctuary, Elle." Robyn's voice was thick, she was obviously on the verge of tears. "Griff chased them off."

"The dogs?" I gasped.

"They're all fine. They were in the kitchen with Robyn," Griff assured us.

"Is the sanctuary destroyed?" Davy sounded defeated, as if all the life had been crushed out of him.

"The fire didn't have time to take hold," Griff said. "One pen is blackened. I can repair the damage easy enough."

"Did you catch the arsonist?" I asked.

"No." Griff sounded as grim as I'd ever heard him. "We've called the sheriff's office. They're on their way."

"They're not gonna stop, are they, Davy?"

Robyn said. "They want to destroy us."

I heard Robyn start sobbing and Griff trying to soothe her.

Davy looked up at me. "It's got to be Charlie Reedham."

He was probably right although we couldn't jump to conclusions. I couldn't afford to accuse an important man like Reedham. Yes, as a Ralston I could bury him, but I didn't want to be that kind of person. I didn't want to be like my grandfather. If I found out he was responsible for the fire though, six feet under wouldn't be deep enough to hide from me.

"I'm on my way home, Robyn. Take care of her, Griff."

"I will," Griff said.

Davy looked as grim as I'd ever seen him. "I need to get home, Elle."

"The SUV is waiting," I said. "I'm coming too."

He took my hands and held them tight. "I think you ought to go home. I can't take the risk of you being hurt."

"There's no way I'm leaving you to face this alone."

"No, Elle, I don't want you at the farm with an arsonist about. Griff will agree with me."

My jaw dropped open. "You're trying to push me away? After everything I've done for you?"

He stiffened, his face going cold, and pulled away from me. "I didn't realize your help came with conditions."

I furrowed my brow. "What are you talking about?"

"You think I'm your lapdog? Your pet to walk at your heel? That's not a marriage, Elle. I'm the owner of the farm and I was going to be your husband."

I latched onto the one word that made sense. "Was?"

Chapter 25

Davy

At Elle's distraught expression, full eyes, and quivering bottom lip, I felt as if my heart were breaking in two. I leaned back so I couldn't be tempted to touch her and my resolve fail.

"I can't be your husband if you don't have any respect for me, Elle. A man can only have his pride trampled on so much before he snaps, and I've reached that point."

"But I do respect you," she insisted.

"Do you?" I asked gently. The last thing I wanted to do was upset her, but she needed to understand how I felt. "From the moment I met you again, I've been on a rollercoaster. You did everything I didn't want. From paying the feed bills to clearing the mortgage. And I'm grateful. I really am. But you've got to understand how I feel, Elle. Since I met you, I've had no control over my life. I'm a proud man but I'm worn down. If our relationship is all about you jerking me around on a piece of string, that's no relationship at all."

Elle looked down at the emerald ring on her finger and twisted it around. "I didn't think I was doing that."

"I told you I didn't want to owe the Ralston family anything. I told you why. I bared my soul to you. But you ignored me and instead I owe the Ralstons everything."

"They owed you, Davy. You didn't deserve what my family did to you."

"No, I didn't," I agreed. "And I'll never forgive them. But I don't want to be in debt to them—you."

"I saved your farm."

"I know. And I'm grateful."

"Are you? Because it sounds like you're resentful." Elle had put her finger on the heart of the matter.

"I am," I admitted. "But not for the reason you think."

"I don't know what you're thinking, Davy," she said, now sounding exasperated.

I huffed and scrubbed my fingers through my hair. "I'm a traditional man. I thought I'd have the kind of marriage my parents did."

"You expect to give the orders?" she sneered. "You want to keep me barefoot and in the kitchen."

I gave her a disappointed look and she had the grace to look away. "I thought we'd have a partnership. Like Momma and my Daddy."

"I'm sorry. That was disrespectful to your parents. I want that kind of relationship too."

"But you keep making decisions for me."

"Is that so bad? I saved the farm."

"Maybe that's the problem," I said as gently as I could. "I want a partner and you want someone you can manage."

She huffed in annoyance. "I can't change who I am, Davy. I'll always be a Ralston."

"I hoped you'd become a Jenner." I looked at the ring on her finger. "I'm going home, Elle. Decide what you want from us. But I'm not settling for second best. I'll never be your lap dog. Everyone has a breaking point." I echoed her words. "I've reached mine."

And I walked to the door of the plane without looking back, just as I had ten years ago.

Was I a fool? I didn't know. But I knew there was some things worth fighting for and how our relationship worked was one of them.

I leaned against the railing, Bailey at my feet, both of us watching the horses run and jump like foals, rather than the sedate mares they actually were. Something had gotten into them this evening and it was good to see. Even Peardrop was playing with the other horses, rather than finding a corner to be by herself. She'd taken time to settle into the new barn, but the other two mares seemed to understand she needed gentle handling. I agreed with Leo's assessment though. She could never be adopted. Peardrop was part of our family for the rest of her life.

"They're happy this evening," Griff remarked as he joined me.

"It's good to see," I said.

"Peardrop too."

I grunted, and we both watched the horses until they decided they'd had enough and went back to lipping lazily at the grass.

I got the feeling Griff had something to say. I had a fair idea what it could be, but I decided to let Griff take his own time and say what he had to.

"You've been kind letting me into your family," he said finally.

I turned to look at him, but Griff was still staring at the horses. "Spit it out, man," I said, forgetting my earlier thought of letting him take his time.

He snorted and huffed, but he turned and leaned his back against the railing, his thumbs in his waistband.

"Robyn's been talking to Elle."

"I thought she might," I said calmly.

"Did you break it off because you were angry with her, or because you didn't want her to be in danger?"

I said nothing. He grunted as if that were answer enough.

It had been two days since I'd gotten home and told them the wedding was off—probably. Then I said I didn't want to talk about it and I needed to repair the sanctuary.

But Griff's assessment was right. It didn't take long to repair the damaged pen. Sheriff Hernández was still looking for the arsonist, but Griff's contacts had told him Charlie Reedham was right there at the top of the suspects list.

"Would you give me your blessing to marry Robyn?" he asked finally.

"Yeah."

Griff turned to look at me. "Yeah? Does that mean you're okay with it?"

I shrugged. "What do you want me to say? You love my sister. She loves you. Treat her kindly and with respect or you'll regret it."

"But—"

"If you're expecting me to say something flowery, you'll be waiting a long time," I said. "You've got my blessing. What more do you want?"

I heard a snort behind me and turned to see Robyn grinning at me. Of course Gizmo was in Robyn's arms and Bella and Miles followed behind them.

"I told you that's what he'd say," Robyn said, hurrying over to Griff to hug him.

Griff threw his hands up in the air. I still wasn't sure what I missed. I'd said yes. What more did the man want?

"Did you ask him about the animal sanctuary?" Robyn asked.

"Give me a break," he grumbled. "I haven't gotten that far yet."

She knit her brows. "What have you been talking about?"

"The horses," he said.

Robyn looked at him as if he were crazy.

"What about the animal sanctuary?" I intervened. "Is something else wrong?" I didn't think I could take another problem. My nerves were frayed as it was.

Griff exchanged a look with Robyn who gave him a nod. Waiting for him to speak tightened my nerves.

"I'd like to take over running the animal

sanctuary."

I furrowed my brow. "Aren't you the head of Elle's protection detail?"

"I want to resign and move here to be with Robyn." Griff exhaled. "Look, you have the farm, and it takes all your time. I know how hard you work. Robyn is spending more time working with Justin. She's good at it too. Neither of you have time to focus on the animal sanctuary. These guys..." He bent down to scratch behind Bella's ears and pat Miles on the head. "They deserve undivided attention. It's okay when we've just got a few dogs, but what happens when we're full?" Bella leaned into him in ecstasy.

I was aware of two pairs of eyes fixed on me. The dogs were looking elsewhere. The horses were more interested in the grass.

"I know what you're saying, but how are we gonna pay you? We can barely afford to keep the farm going even with Elle's help."

I was relieved when I managed to say her name calmly and without breaking down. I really needed *not* to be the bad guy in this discussion.

"I've got savings," Griff said. He didn't seem surprised or offended by the question. "I've never spent a lot. I want to be a partner in your business. Then we can rethink if the animal sanctuary isn't paying its way. And you need help on the farm, especially now Robyn is working for Justin full-time."

I stared at him. "What?" Robyn groaned and I turned on her. "When were you going to tell me?"

"I've been working for him since the auction,"

Robyn grumbled. "I charged them by the hour. Elle just wants to make it official. No one's got time to handle the work for the new foundation, so that's going to be me."

I closed my eyes and gave a disbelieving laugh. I'd spent years hating the Ralstons and now I couldn't get away from them.

"Davy, I won't do this if you don't want me to," Robyn said.

I opened my eyes. She looked so worried. "This is not my decision, Robyn. You're a big girl now. No matter what my issues with the Ralstons I would never stand in the way of your career." I heard a relieved sigh from Griff. "You guys have got to stop treating me as if I'll fall apart if I hear the Ralston name. I've gotten over that."

Robyn gave me the 'I know you're talking out of your butt' look she'd perfected from Momma. But she focused on herself, not me, to my relief.

"I've been working for Justin and he's the one who asked me to work full time. I just said yes five minutes ago. You'll need Griff. You can't manage the farm and the sanctuary. He'll be living here. Let him invest in Black Feather farm. We worked out all the figures. This is feasible."

I nodded. Of course they had. If they were going to get wed it made sense, even if he wasn't a Jenner. This was business. I needed Griff's help and if it didn't work out, then we'd make other arrangements. I glanced around them all. "No more secrets."

"No more secrets," they echoed together.

"But what are you going to do about Elle?"

Robyn asked. "The wedding is supposed to be in three weeks."

I huffed, really not wanting to have this conversation, and knowing I couldn't avoid it. "I don't know. I left it in Elle's hands."

"You walked out on her," Robyn said. "Again."

"You know why I left," I said.

Robyn nodded. "I understand, but Davy, are you willing to sacrifice the woman you've loved for half your life for the sake of your pride?"

"It's not just pride, Robyn. I want a relationship like Momma's and Daddy's. Can I really have that with Elsa Ralston? Will she understand when I want to protect her? Will she listen when I say no?"

Robyn crossed her arms and glowered at me. "How do you know? You walked out on her—again."

I turned back to the horses. What was the point? I had nothing left to say. Then I felt Robyn lean against my back and hug me close.

"I'm sorry, Davy. That was mean. I just want her back, you know?"

I hugged her arms. "Me too, Robyn. Me too."

"So what are you going to do about it?"

"I really don't know," I admitted.

Chapter 26

Elle

I stayed in Boston for two weeks. Robyn told me Davy was moping and when was I going to come home and fix it. My mom couldn't hide her smug expression. I had a long lunch with Lily and spilled out everything Davy and I had said. I thought she would take my side. As a Duchamp I thought she'd understand.

Instead, she studied me for a long time. "You're miserable."

"Yes."

"He's miserable."

"Yes."

"So what are you going to do about it?"

"He's the one who walked away," I said indignantly.

"He went home. Someone just tried to burn down that animal sanctuary. You know, the one we put all the time and energy into rebuilding."

I stared into my glass of wine. "I thought you'd be on my side."

Lily reached over and held my hand. "Which side is that, Elle? The one where you're rich, proud, and miserable, and think you're right? Or the one where you're happily married to the man you've loved forever, and you listen to him, and he listens to you. Sometimes you argue. Like partners do."

"You don't take any prisoners," I muttered.

"Not when I'm talking to two people who should know better."

I looked up and Lily's smirk was wide. "You've spoken to Davy?"

"Yes. And gave him the same lecture."

"What did he say?" I knew I sounded pathetic.

"I'm not going to repeat it. But he did tell me to leave you alone." Lily smirked again.

"Glad to see you took his advice."

Lily shrugged. "You asked for my advice. You don't have to like it. So what are you going to do?"

I threw back the wine. "I'm going to get my man. Do you have a lasso?"

Lily nodded at me approvingly. "Go get your man! And if he doesn't listen, get the handcuffs to cuff him to the nearest tree."

I thought that sounded like an excellent plan.

I found Davy sitting by the creek. Not at sunrise. He'd just come out there to think. I could tell by the way he stared into the long distance.

I sat down beside him, and he wrapped his arm around me. I rested my head on his shoulder.

"If you have me, I'll never walk away from you again," he said.

"The next time you try will be the last," I warned. "I have my limits too."

"Understood."

"And I can't promise not to go all Elsa on you, but if you hate it, I'll listen. I want to be your partner until we're old and gray."

"I like that idea," Davy said. "Partners for life."

We put the wedding off for a few more weeks. Davy and I were working through things and my work was still hectic. Griff was busy with the sanctuary too. But also because the sheriff turned up one day to tell us Charlie Reedham had been arrested and he'd confessed not only to starting the second fire, but also starting the first. He'd barely escaped with his life that time, the fire had taken ahold so quickly.

It was then Davy told me about the cable he and Greg had found. I was hurt he had told Griff but not me. Then he told me that Reedham's threats had scared him. He didn't want to take any chances with me or Robyn. I saw the pain in his eyes and didn't press him. Reedham's confession hit Davy and Robyn hard. The man had killed their Momma. They would always believe that.

It was a chilly morning, and we were all dressed in jackets and hats, our breaths visible as we spoke. But the day promised to be a fine one. Just right for the first day of our marriage.

I stood by Davy's side clutching his hand tightly as the officiant said the few words needed to make us man and wife. It was here Davy had first told me he loved me, and it was here he promised to be my husband and stay by my side forever. His vows were sweet and simple and mine were the same. I promised to be his wife and listen to him. Neither of us were flowery. We loved each other and that was all that mattered.

Then we turned to face the few people we wanted here. Robyn and Griff, Lily and Greg, and Marisa and her friend, Roman. I'd asked my parents. My mom had sniffed and said she'd wait until we did it properly. But my father had said he wouldn't miss his little girl getting married and he came with Justin. Eight people shared our joy, and it couldn't have been better.

"Where are you taking me for our honeymoon?" Davy asked as we climbed in the SUV.

I grinned at him. "It's a surprise."

"The others know, don't they?" he groused. "They were all smirking at me as they left."

He'd once confessed he'd never been out of the county, let alone the state, and he'd never had a vacation. He'd flown to Boston several times now, although as he pointed out, he'd never seen Boston beyond the airport and Ralston House. He still wasn't comfortable picking a place for a vacation.

I'd promised him we would honeymoon in so many places. A European city, a tropical beach, or sunset atop the Empire State Building in New York. Or all of them. He'd turned to me and said he didn't mind where we were as long as we were together. There was a long pause. Then he winked and added home was where we belonged. I rolled my eyes. My man would always be a home boy.

I rested my head on his shoulder as we drove away from the farm, feeling the tension in his muscles. The handcuffs, except for Griff, would be coming with us. They'd been fully briefed where we were going and asked to stay out of sight as much as possible.

Davy sighed and kissed the top of my head. "I never thought I'd see you again, let alone be lucky enough to marry you."

"I never stopped thinking about you," I confessed. "No one ever matched up to you."

"You mean you never found another grumpy, prickly man like me?"

I grinned at his teasing tone. "You got it. You're perfect for me."

"And you're the only woman I ever loved," he said, and gave me a kiss to prove it.

I wanted to keep him occupied so I told him how sad I was to sell my landscaping business, but two employees had bought it and business was flourishing.

"Why did you start a landscaping business?" Davy asked.

We'd never really had much time to talk about the past ten years. Between the Ralston business, the animal sanctuary, and the farm, the time we'd been apart had been left behind.

"To annoy my mom," I admitted. I gave a wry chuckle. "And at that point college would've been difficult for Dad to finance and the thought of all that debt..." I shuddered.

"Would you like to go back to school now?"

I thought about it for a long moment. "No, I don't think so. I think I've gained life experience. I learned so much from starting a new business from the ground up and on my own. There were times when I thought about walking away, but I was never going to give my family the satisfaction of saying I told you so. It's stood me in good stead for becoming the CEO. Nothing phases me anymore."

"It's like running the farm. You can't afford to panic. You just have to get on with it." Davy looked out of the window and then gave me a puzzled frown. "This isn't the way to the airport."

"I know," I said airily. "We've got a stop to make before we reach the airport."

Davy narrowed his eyes. "I sense you're not telling me the truth. Like that time you said you'd been at Mary Ann's to study but you'd gone to town to buy me a birthday present. You didn't even like Mary Ann."

I gave him a wide-eyed stare, but he just grew more suspicious. I knew I couldn't deceive him for long. He'd always been able to tell. But it didn't matter now. We were nearly there.

We turned off the highway and drove down the narrow road. Davy stared out of the window. "This is Wildcat ranch. What are we doing here?"

I laid my hand on his arm and smiled at him. "Just wait a few minutes and I'll tell you. I promise."

He grunted, but he didn't push me. The SUV halted and one of the guys in front jumped out to open my door. I slid out and looked up at the ranch. It was a pretty two-story building, much larger than the farmhouse.

Davy walked around to join me. "Are you gonna tell me why we're standing outside Charlie Reedham's place?"

I noticed the handcuffs vanish. I snorted. Cowards!

"Well?" he demanded.

I took a deep breath. "We're not standing outside Reedham's home. Wildcat ranch is our new home. Yours and mine. The ranch and the land. So you can expand the farm and the sanctuary if you want."

"You bought me a home?" he asked in a strangled tone.

I shook my head. "I bought *us* a home, which means Griff and Robyn can have the farmhouse to start their married lives. Can you imagine the four of us living in the small house?"

Davy still looked shellshocked. "But this is the Reedham's ranch."

"Jo Beth and her momma are mortified by what Charlie did. If they could make it up to you, they would. Charlie's going to jail, Davy. They just want to get away from here and make a fresh start. I offered them a more than fair price and Griff and Greg helped them move across state. They've gotten a lovely place near Houston."

"But—"

"We needed a home," I pleaded. I didn't want to start our married life fighting over our home.

He folded his arms across his chest and fixed me with his piercing gaze. I felt as if I'd been sent to the principal's office. "If I hadn't told you that story about me wanting to buy the place, would you have considered buying it?"

I nodded. This was a question I could answer. "It makes sense, Davy. It borders Black Feather. I can work from here. Behind the ranch are barns converted into offices. Robyn has already picked one for herself. And there's plenty of room for the horses. Lemondrop and Raindrop are already trying out their new stalls. And there's an airstrip. It needs work but I can fly in and out. I can live here and work. And you can expand the farm if you want to." The words tumbled out as I tried to convince him what a good idea it had been to purchase the ranch. "And Justin says he still wants to learn to ride a horse." I'd finally found out what he and Davy had been discussing in my office. But would Davy agree to the ranch? He was so quiet.

Finally, he huffed out a breath. "You and I are going to have a long chat about you making decisions without me. I thought we'd talked about this."

I nodded. "No more, I promise. And if you hate it, we'll sell it."

He grunted as though he didn't believe me. "So where are we going to have the honeymoon?"

I bit my lip. "Here."

His eyes grew comically wide. "What?"

"You and me. Alone in the ranch. Riding over the land. Making plans for our future. We can go somewhere else if you'd prefer," I said anxiously when he didn't speak.

"You thought I'd like to spend our honeymoon close to home?"

I nodded, aware I'd probably just made a crushing error.

Suddenly, I was swept off my feet into his arms, held close against his chest. I yelped and wrapped my arms around his neck.

"I couldn't think of a honeymoon I'd like better, Mrs. Jenner," he said, and pressed his lips on mine. When he raised his head, he looked at the ranch. "Is the door open?"

I nodded. "We have food for the week. The beds are made. The only thing we need to do is take care of the horses and Robyn says she'll do that if we ask."

Davy's smile was brighter than the sun. "I think we can manage the horses. But first, I'm going to carry you over the threshold of my new home.

I held on tight as he carried me into the kitchen. Davy didn't put me down, just pushing the door closed with one foot.

"I love you, Elsa Jenner," he said as he lowered me to the ground.

"Likewise, David Jenner. Likewise."

And I waited for him to kiss me again.

Epilogue

Davy

I stood by the side of my wife and watched as she cut the ribbon to the Susan Jenner Animal Sanctuary and declared it officially open. We'd been married for two months. I felt as if we'd been together for a lifetime. The Boston wedding hadn't happened yet. That was taking longer to organize. Which was just fine with Elle and me.

On one side of the yard, Robyn curled into Griff's arms and sobbed against his chest. He hugged her tightly and I knew my sister was in good hands. I wasn't far from tears myself and I wished Momma could have been here to see her dream realized. I hoped and prayed she could look down on us and be happy.

I tried not to blink at the barrage of flashlights as the media took endless photos of Elsa Ralston and her friends. It was like a who's who of the Boston wealthy. Thankfully they were all returning home except for Greg and Lily, and Greg's grandmother, who were staying with us in our new home.

Everyone clapped and the rescued dogs howled in accompaniment. I grimaced at the noise. We were almost full-to-capacity already despite the fact we'd only just officially opened.

Griff was already muttering about building more pens. I left it in his hands. The Ralston Foundation had agreed to sponsor us on an ongoing basis, so funding wasn't an issue. We were lucky, I knew that.

Griff moved forward to show people around the sanctuary. We hoped some dogs would be going home with new owners today. Those that had expressed interest had already been checked. Griff insisted on that, and no one said no to Griff.

I'd stepped back from the animal sanctuary and focused my attention on the farm and the ranch. Elle and I had stayed at the ranch to give Robyn and Griff the farmhouse. Their wedding wasn't until the end of the month, so Griff shared the bunkhouse with the new handcuffs while he repainted and updated the interior of the house. He had officially resigned as head of Elle's protection detail.

Robyn came over and hugged me so fiercely I protested I needed to breathe. She ignored me and hugged me again.

"It's open, Davy. Momma would be so proud."

"She would," I agreed, all choked up.

So much had changed in the past year. We'd hit rock bottom hard and now we were on top of the world.

Robyn hugged Elle and I heard whispering, but neither of them cared to share it with me. Then Robyn returned to Griff and Elle snuggled into my side.

I bent to kiss her lips. "Thank you for loving me," I murmured. I could have thanked her for so many things but loving me came top of the list.

She gave me a brilliant smile. "I never stopped."

My heart skipped a beat. I was such a lucky man.

Elle leaned forward. "Tomorrow morning do you think we could watch the sunrise?"

I hugged her close to me. "That sounds like an excellent idea."

Then we were surrounded by the media wanting to know how Elle had gotten involved. I let her handle the explanations. She was a master at dealing with the press by this time. As much as I still had resentment against her grandfather, choosing Elle to be the face of the company had been a masterstroke.

Then Elle got a break long enough to hug Lily and Greg. One day I'd find a way to thank them for the work they'd put in to help the animal sanctuary.

Elle hugged Lily while I shook Greg's hand.

"You're finally officially open," Greg said to me.

"It was a race whether we were gonna be full before the big day," I admitted. "We could be ten times the size and still not have enough space."

His eyes lit up. Greg had confessed that building the sanctuary had been the most fun and satisfaction he'd had in years.

"Talk to Griff," I said. "He's already talking about extending the pens."

Lily groaned as our wives turned to us. "Don't encourage him. Greg's already talking about building a sanctuary by us."

Greg smirked at me.

"I thought you were starting your research," Elle said.

"I am," he protested, "but I liked the physical work, and seeing the animals as happy as they can be, is so worth it."

Lily wrapped her arm around Greg's waist and smiled up at him. "You can do whatever you want."

He dropped a kiss on her lips then smiled at us. "I'm so lucky."

We both were very lucky guys.

Sheriff Hernández took me to one side during the afternoon. My stomach did an unpleasant flop as I wondered what bad news would manage to spoil our day.

"Charlie Reedham has changed his plea to guilty," he said.

I took a deep breath. "That means there's no trial?"

Hernández nodded. "He's due to be sentenced next week, but you don't have to be there."

I took off my hat and scrubbed my fingers through my hair. "What changed his mind?"

The sheriff gave me a thin smile. "The evidence keeps piling up thanks to his friends. I think his lawyers convinced him he'd get a reduced sentence if he admitted his guilt than risk going to trial."

"I'm glad," I said honestly. "I don't think me and Robyn could take reliving that night again."

Hernández squeezed my shoulder. "Enjoy your fresh start."

A short, attractive woman with glossy black hair and dark eyes joined us, holding a leash to one of our longest residents, the elderly tan pitbull with a tail that never stopped wagging.

"Bella." I bent to scratch her behind the ears. She closed her eyes and smiled in ecstasy. "I'm sad to see you go, girl, but you're going to a great home."

Hernández groaned. "We don't need another dog."

His wife scowled at him. "She is perfect. She will fit right in."

I could have suggested the sheriff gave it up as a lost cause. His three kids squealed as they ran over, and Bella was drowned in a happy sea of hugs and kisses. I kept a close eye on how she reacted, ready to calm things down if she showed any signs of fear or uncertainty, but as usual, the dog reveled in all the attention.

The sheriff scowled at me. I grinned at him. He sighed and bent to love on Bella who stared up at him with adoration.

The family walked away, Bella by the sheriff's heels. I wondered how long it would be before I saw her in his police vehicle.

I exhaled as I thought about the news he'd just given me. That was a relief. I thought about going to the sentencing and decided I didn't care enough. He would be going to jail. I had better things to focus on.

As much as the day was emotional and

amazing, it was a relief when all the people and over half the dogs went home, including Miles, the nervous Labrador. He'd gone home with an army vet who'd told me he knew just how Miles felt. They could heal each other. He'd also offered to volunteer at the sanctuary. That left eight of us, plus Gizmo and Bailey, sitting around the table eating chicken pot pie. Marisa and Roman, Greg, and Griff were deeply involved in a discussion about wood turning of all things, while Robyn and Lily seemed to be making plans for another fundraising event.

Elle leaned against me, and I noticed she'd not eaten much, just pushing the food around her plate.

"Are you all right?" I asked, concerned because Elle had always loved Momma's chicken pot pie.

"I'm just not hungry," she admitted, and I noticed how pale she looked. "I think it's been a long day. I'll feel better in the morning."

I brushed her hair in a brief kiss. "I'll take you home soon."

"I forgot to ask. What did the sheriff want?"

I relayed our conversation and everyone around the table stopped to listen. I saw the relief on Robyn's face, and she pressed in close to Griff.

"I hope they lock Reedham up and throw away the key," Griff growled.

No one disagreed.

"Jo Beth Reedham contacted me to apologize again," Robyn said. "She and her momma are glad to be away from here."

I wasn't surprised. I'd heard the gossip

spreading like wildfire through the community. "We can make sure they get the help they need." Reedham was one thing, but his kin didn't deserve to suffer.

Griff nodded. "We can do that."

Elle pressed a kiss to my jaw. "You're all so kind."

I hugged her to me. "Not everyone is as lucky as us."

We didn't manage to ride out to the creek every day, but enough to keep us both happy. The mares were stabled at the ranch now as Griff and Robyn didn't have much time for riding. The fact Griff turned pale every time he looked at a horse was irrelevant, or so he kept telling me.

It took longer to get to the creek now, and we sneaked out of the house early so we didn't disturb our guests. We still liked watching the sun rise in our place. Bailey raised his head from his place by the stove as we left, but subsided with a huff when I told him no.

I hugged Elle close to me as we watched the first peek of the orange glow on the horizon. "I love you." I'd never stop telling her that as long as I lived.

The sun's rays bathed Elle's face as she sighed and turned to me. "I've got something to tell you."

"There's no more room for another horse," I said promptly.

She rolled her eyes. "It's an addition to the farm, but it's not a horse."

"You want the alpaca, don't you?"

Elle laid her hand over my mouth. "Hush."

I nodded and she took her hand away. Then she took my hand and laid it on her flat belly. I stared at her, and her smile was brighter than any sun.

"What do you think about a fall baby?" Elle asked.

"Are you sure?" I managed, my voice hoarse.

"I'm sure," she said. "I did another test when I got up. You're going to be a daddy."

I did the only thing a man could do in the face of such news. I put my head on her shoulder and sobbed. Elle held me tight and crooned in my ear. When I'd gotten myself under control, I raised my head and kissed my wife until we were both breathless.

"Do you want a boy or a girl?" she asked.

"Yes," I said.

Elle laughed. "That's the right answer."

I looked down at her. "What about your job? Do you want to return to Boston?"

Elle looked horrified. "No way. I'm having my baby right here on the farm."

"But you still have to deal with the family business."

"I've been thinking about that."

Of course she had. My girl had probably worked out every conceivable problem and come up with solutions to all of them.

"I think it's time Justin got a promotion, don't you?"

I furrowed my brow. "You want him to become the face of the Ralston empire? Don't you have to be a Ralston?"

"Yes, but he can handle all the firefighting without me being there. The board keep trying to poach him from me. If I make him VP in charge of problem solving, they might leave him alone. What do you think?"

"I think the man deserves triple the salary plus extra zeros."

Poor guy. Poor poor guy.

"Already in hand," she said with a smirk. "I'm thinking of asking Robyn to become my assistant. She's been well trained by Justin. I'm taking maternity leave and my job will be divided between Justin and my father, if they both agree."

I hummed and kissed her again. Robyn and Justin would relish the opportunity. Edward, I was sure, just wanted to go fishing.

But solving that was for another day. I wanted to focus on the woman in my arms and the gift she'd given me.

A new baby. I thought of a small kid running next to Bailey over our land. Another generation of Ralstons. I snorted. And Jenners. Who'd have believed it?

The next book, *Sunset Behind Lavender Cottage*, will be out 2021

He tells me to jump. Behind me are snooty guys with their eyes on my new fortune.

Below me is a handsome man who promises to catch me. What do I do?
Rowan has lived her entire life in Boston, barely making her rent each month. Now she's the heiress to some crusty estate in England because her great-grandfather wants to clear his conscience about the way he treated Rowan's grandmother.
Rowan is not just wealthy beyond her wildest dreams, she's inherited a title to boot.
She makes the trip to her new home, only to discover she is now the bait in a lake of sharks. Then one man offers to hide her.

Also by Emma Lewis.

You can find all of Emma's books over at Amazon. Don't forget to sign up for her newsletter. https://landing.mailerlite.com/webforms/landing/u4n6w6?

About Emma Lewis

Emma is new to this genre, but not to writing romance. It's her joy to make two people live happily ever after. She hopes one day it will happen to her, but in the meantime, she shares her life with her dog and her collection of arc deco lamps.

Come over and talk to Emma at:
Newsletter:
https://landing.mailerlite.com/webforms/landing/u4n6w6?
Author group – Facebook:
https://www.facebook.com/groups/394860531894731
Facebook:
https://www.facebook.com/emmalewisromance/
Email: emmalewisromance@gmail.com

* 9 7 9 8 4 8 4 8 9 6 4 7 9 *